You Have to Stop This

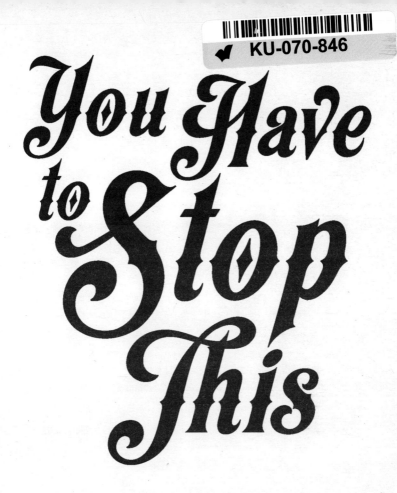

By
Pseudonymous Bosch

USBORNE

The Oath of Terces

I have a Secret I can't
tell nor ink.
Though it has no scent,
it does often stink.
Though it makes no sound,
it can make you roar.
When it's tasteless,
I like it all the more.
Though it has no shade,
it lacks not colour.
Though it has no shape,
no cause for dolour.
If you think you know it, you're incorrect,
And from you the Secret
I will protect.
The Secret of Life is not stone nor cents,
For the Secret Sense is
but a nonsense.

Egypt, 1212BC

An ibis stood, silent and still, on the shore of the Nile.

Below him, birds dived into the river's murky shallows, vainly stabbing at frogs and fish. Occasionally, one or two rose victorious out of the water, dangling their dripping prey from their beaks. The other birds squawked in jealousy. But the ibis – the sacred ibis, as the Egyptian variety of the species is known – seemed unaware of the commotion around him.

With his snow-white body, ink-black head, and long, curved beak, he looked proud, elegant, inscrutable.

He took no notice of the villagers washing their linens on the rocks. Nor of the fishermen passing by in their reed boats. When children threw stones at the other birds, they flapped their wings in fright; the ibis kept his wings closed around his body like a shell. Only the brief appearance of a crocodile crawling through the papyrus plants caused the ibis's feathers to ruffle; and even then, his stick-like legs never moved.

For hours, the ibis stared unwaveringly at the horizon. It was as if he were waiting for a signal – a red flag, say, or a puff of smoke – but the sun set, the moon rose, the stars twinkled, and still he did not stir.

Then, well after more cautious birds had retired to their nests, the ibis suddenly and without warning spread his wings and jumped into the air. He flew swiftly and purposefully across the Nile, his slender neck stretched forward into the night, his wide, white wings illuminated from behind by the brilliant light of the Saharan moon.

Elsewhere in the desert, on the steep stone steps of a temple to the god Thoth, an innocent man was being executed by order of the pharaoh.

There was no way the ibis could have heard the condemned man's cries, let alone have read the fateful secret the man had inscribed only a moment before on a piece of papyrus. And yet it almost seemed the ibis was heeding his call.

CHAPTER
ONE

P ick one:*

a) A short time ago, in a land uncomfortably close by...
b) He was a dark and stormy knight.
c) He was the best of mimes. He was the worst of mimes.
d) This book looks lame. I'm watching TV.
e) Run!

---

*THE CORRECT ANSWER IS *E) RUN!*, AS IN *RUN AWAY FROM THIS BOOK RIGHT NOW IF YOU KNOW WHAT'S GOOD FOR YOU.*

The Fire Sale

Okay, you've waited long enough. Let me put you out of your misery right now.

I will reveal the Secret – a secret that people have sought for centuries, for millennia even – on the very next page...

Well, maybe the next page...

The next . . . ?

No, no, I can't. It's much too soon.

If I tell you the Secret now, you won't want to read any further, will you?

I'll do it before the end of this book.

I promise.

Maybe.

It depends on a few things.

For instance – how you look at it.

Are you really sure you want to know the Secret, anyway?

Revealing a secret is a bit like releasing air from a balloon: the secret spirals around and makes a fun noise – and if you aim right, it might even hit somebody in the nose – but afterwards it always falls to the ground, and everyone is left with that sad, after-the-balloon feeling of loss and abandonment.

That doesn't sound very satisfying, does it?

Then again, when have you known me to satisfy anything but my own cravings for chocolate?

Honestly, I don't know why you bother to read a word I write. If you want to give up on me now, I understand completely. Never mind all the time you've already put in; sometimes it's better to cut and run (see Chapter One).

Now's your chance to escape. Don't worry – I won't look. I'll just close my eyes and have a nibble of this delicious bar of dark, dark—

Hmmgh . . . well, maybe just one more . . . *hmmgh . . .*

—No? You're staying put? Stubborn, aren't you? Or just morbidly curious?

I know, this book is like a car accident. You don't *want* to stare – you just can't help it.

If it's any comfort, your old friend Cass is anything but satisfied at the time this story begins. She, too, is desperate to learn the Secret.

Recently, remember, she came torturously close to learning the Secret. Among the things she inherited from her ancestor, the Jester, was a fragment of papyrus with the Secret written on it in hieroglyphs. Alas, the papyrus disintegrated in front of her eyes.

Now Cass is headed for her grandfathers' place. She has just heard that her grandfathers are selling their old firehouse, and she wants to make sure the Jester's trunk doesn't get lost in the move. She hopes that another clue about the Secret may lie inside the—

*   *   *

Oh! There she is, walking down the road to the firehouse with Max-Ernest. I didn't realize I'd been going on for so long.

If I'm not mistaken, they are discussing the assignment they just handed in for their class's Egypt unit: *make a list of the ten things you would take with you into the afterlife.* As I'm sure you know, the ancient Egyptians were very keen on keeping as many of their possessions as possible – for as long as possible.

Here, let's listen:

"...and a giant bar of chocolate, of course, in case I get hungry in the afterlife, and a pair of underwear, because, you know," Max-Ernest was saying. "Oh, and a deck of cards. Or do you think that's cheating? Since there are fifty-two cards in a deck, and we're only supposed to take ten things?"

"No, I think you can count a deck as one thing," said Cass, walking a little way ahead. Max-Ernest struggled to keep up.

The view couldn't have been more familiar. The backpack. The braids. The big pointy ears. Always, always from behind. Which was very unfair, when you thought about it. He, Max-Ernest, was shorter than Cass. Rightfully, he should go first; he wouldn't block her line of vision.

"Did the Egyptians have cards?" Cass asked casually.

"It seems like hieroglyphs would make a cool deck of cards."

Max-Ernest lit up. "That's a great idea! I don't think the Egyptians had them, but we could make our own cards and —"

"There are just twenty-four hieroglyphs in the Egyptian alphabet, right?" asked Cass, cutting him off. "Or are there more? I feel like I heard both things."

Cass stopped at a junction. Cars passed at a snail's pace, honking their horns impatiently. It was unexpectedly busy for their quiet neighbourhood.

"Well, there are twenty-four main ones. They stand in for sounds, like our letters do," Max-Ernest explained, happy to discuss a topic that was of such passionate interest to him. "But there are thousands and thousands of others that are more like picture-words. I don't think anybody knows how many —"

Cass's face fell. "They don't?"

"Yeah, think about it – your card deck could be as big as you want," said Max-Ernest enthusiastically.

"Oh no. That's just what I was afraid of..."

Max-Ernest looked at Cass, confused by her sudden change of mood. "What do you mean? Why is that a bad thing?"

Cass bit her lip. She was the Secret Keeper; the Secret was supposed to be hers alone. Not to mention, it was common knowledge that Max-Ernest couldn't keep a secret. And yet, despite his faults, he was her best friend and unflagging investigative companion. She'd been resisting for weeks, but she couldn't help wanting to confide in him.

She looked at her friend and took the plunge. "What if I told you I got the Jester's trunk open?"

Max-Ernest's eyes widened. "You figured out the combination?"

Cass nodded. "And what if I told you there was a piece of papyrus inside, with writing on it?"

"With hieroglyphs, you mean? That's why you're asking about them?"

Cass didn't say anything.

Max-Ernest stared at her. "Wait – this doesn't have anything to do with the Secret, does it?"

"Shh!! What are you thinking—?!"

They both looked around. Nobody was within earshot. (You and me they couldn't see, of course.)

"Sorry," said Max-Ernest, red-faced.

Not mentioning the Secret aloud was one of the most important rules – almost the only rule – for members of their secret organization, the Terces Society. Normally, even the compulsively talkative Max-Ernest abided by it.

"Anyway, it doesn't matter what it was. It was so

old that it turned to dust as soon as I saw it," said Cass glumly.

"So what you're saying is, you had the you-know-what in your hands, and then it just disappeared?" The full weight of it was sinking into Max-Ernest's head. "That's...that's horrible!"

Cass sighed and started walking across the street. "I promised myself I wouldn't tell you—"

"Don't worry. You didn't tell me – I guessed," said Max-Ernest, following her. "Anyway, how could you *not* tell me? I'm the one who knows hieroglyphs. Can you remember any? I could translate them—"

"I know, it's driving me crazy. It's the one time I need your help, and I can't ask—"

"The one time—?"

"You know what I mean."

"No, I don't. You've needed my help exactly six hundred and thirty-two times."

Cass shook her head in amazement. "You've been counting?"

Max-Ernest shrugged off the question. "So what else was in the trunk the Jester sent you, besides the papyrus?"

"Nothing important. Just treasure."

"You mean like *treasure* treasure? Gold coins and stuff?"

"Yeah, a lot, actually," said Cass, as if it were no

big deal. "I want to look again in case there are any other clues in there about...*it*."

"I can't believe you waited so long to tell me all this," said Max-Ernest. "No wonder you've been acting so weird lately. You're...rich."

But Cass wasn't listening; she was staring down the street, where there was a terrible traffic jam. Cars were stalled. People were shouting. Babies were crying.

"What's going on?" she asked, her pointy ears tingling in alarm.

As they got closer to the old firehouse where Cass's grandfathers lived, men and women and children walked by, holding boxes and bags with odd old objects peeking out: a broken banjo, a Hula Hoop, a fireplace poker, a fishing rod, several ancient computers, even a cash register.

"Maybe there's going to be a hurricane or a flood?" suggested Max-Ernest. "Or a big fire?"

Cass, who was normally the one to predict disasters of that sort, shook her head. "Uh, I don't think so. It's...something worse."

"What – nuclear war?"

"No, a garage sale," said Cass grimly.

She was right.

Their progress slowed to a near halt as they came within view of the firehouse. The entire street was crowded with cardboard boxes and people combing through them. Tables were piled high with dusty glassware and broken ceramics and hard-to-identify appliances. Mismatched shoes and neckties of all sizes and colours flew into the air as people discarded them. Old books and magazines covered the ground like fallen leaves.

"Are your grandfathers really selling all their stuff? I can't believe it," said Max-Ernest.

"I know – it's weird," said Cass, slightly nauseated.

She stopped in front of the firehouse, where a new yellow sign had been planted. Instead of a sign for her grandfathers' antiques store, the Fire Sale, there was now one that said

GLORIA FORTUNE
Estate Agent

Cass stared at the sign as if it were an alien spacecraft that had landed on her grandfathers' front steps. "My mom said they were moving, but I guess I didn't really think about what that meant. It's like they're selling my childhood—"

"So where did you leave the trunk?" asked Max-Ernest, who was understandably eager to get his first view of real treasure.

He glanced around. A few trunks lay on the street, but none that looked like the ancient trunk that Cass's ancestor had sent her so many centuries ago – and that had circled the globe so many times before reaching her.

"Huh? Oh, I hid it way in the back." Cass started up the front steps of the firehouse. "Come on, let's go inside before my grandfathers see us."

But when they looked inside, the firehouse was completely empty – that is, aside from the cobwebs and dust that had accumulated behind all the boxes and shelves and tables that had, until very recently, cluttered the space.

The one familiar thing that remained: the brass fire pole, as shiny as ever. Cass swallowed, remembering all the times she had slid down it.

"Um, Cass, shouldn't we go look outside before somebody—?"

"Don't even think it!" said Cass, running out the door.

If they didn't find the trunk before some lucky garage-sale customer snatched it away, Cass's glittering inheritance – not to mention any clue it might contain about the Secret – would be lost for ever.

The Big Stuff

They found Grandpa Larry standing by a table of books.

"How much is this old set?" a scowling man was asking.

"The encyclopedia? Why, it's a classic, and it's not for sale!" said Grandpa Larry automatically.

"Then what's it doing out here?" the customer replied angrily.

"Fine, twist my arm, five dollars," said Grandpa Larry grumpily.

"Eh, maybe I'll just—"

"Oh, heck, twenty-five cents."

"Deal!" The gleeful customer started scooping up encyclopedia volumes and tossing them into a cardboard box.

"Hey, Grandpa Larry." Cass tugged on her grandfather's sleeve. He was wearing a vintage Hawaiian shirt and a Panama hat – as if he were dressed for a tropical vacation.

Grandpa Larry smiled in delight. "Cass! I didn't know you were here."

"Well, I didn't know you were moving!" said Cass accusatorily.

"Didn't your mother tell you? We're going on an around-the-world cruise."

"Cruises are for old people. You hate all that stuff."

"What do you mean? We *are* old people."

"I still don't understand why you have to sell everything. Aren't you going to come back? What about my graduation?"

Grandpa Larry put his arm around Cass. "You know as well as I do, this place hasn't been the same since Sebastian left us," he said gently.

Cass nodded. Six weeks earlier, the ailing basset hound, who had survived long beyond the dire predictions of veterinarians, had died in his sleep. Cass, who loved Sebastian as if he were her own dog, had been unable to bring herself to visit ever since.

"All this stuff – it was bogging us down." Grandpa Larry gestured to the piles around him. "And, besides, you know what they say: you can't take it with you."

While Cass tried to absorb what he was saying, Grandpa Larry turned to Max-Ernest. "Max-Ernest, my friend, anything you want, I'll give you a great deal – it's called *free*," he whispered confidentially. "I have some joke books you'll like. Also, a set of loaded dice—"

"Thanks, Grandpa Larry," said Max-Ernest, wistfully eyeing the tables around him. "But right now, um, Cass has a question."

"Oh yeah," said Cass, who was so upset she'd all but forgotten the purpose of their visit. "Grandpa

Larry, have you seen a big old trunk around – you know, the kind with a lot of travel stickers?"

Larry looked curiously at Cass. "That wasn't yours, was it? We couldn't remember where we picked it up. Figured it must have been one of those lost weekends in the 1970s..."

"Yeah, no, I mean, it's not mine!" said Cass in a rush. "I was just wondering if you had a trunk like that because...because we're doing a unit on ancient Egypt at school, and we're supposed to put together a box of all the stuff we would take into the afterlife."

Grandpa Larry laughed. "After you're mummified, you mean?"

"Exactly," said Cass.

Max-Ernest nodded, playing along. "On Friday, we're going on a field trip to the mummy exhibit at the Natural History Museum." (That part, at least, was true. As for the afterlife assignment, it had been turned in already.)

"Well, the trunk I'm thinking of would be perfect – it's a time capsule all by itself," said Grandpa Larry. "Last I saw, Grandpa Wayne was hauling it outside."

Grandpa Wayne, who was dressed not in tropical finery but in his usual grease-stained mechanic's overalls, was in the middle of explaining the intricacies of repairing a fifty-year-old black-and-white TV to a bored customer. When Cass and Max-Ernest ran up, the customer hurriedly – and gratefully – excused himself.

Grandpa Wayne remembered the trunk – he had spent forty-five minutes trying to open the lock before giving up – but there were so many people coming in and out that he couldn't remember whether he'd sold it or not.

"Try looking by my truck – that's where all the big stuff is."

The "big stuff" lying by Wayne's rusty old truck included such marvels as a purple player piano; a tuba with a small palm tree growing out of it; and a dry aquarium with a miniature pink castle that was home to a family of cockroaches.

Unfortunately, there was no trunk in sight. Cass and Max-Ernest looked around nervously, neither of them voicing their fears.

"What's Sebastian's bed doing here?" asked Max-Ernest, nodding at the threadbare doggy bed lying on the truck's open tailgate.

Nestled on the bed was a ceramic cookie jar shaped like a bone. Next to the bed was a sign: NOT FOR SALE.

Cass bent down and sniffed Sebastian's bed. "It smells like him."

Max-Ernest lifted the lid of the cookie jar, then quickly closed it.

"What – mouldy biscuits or something?" asked Cass.

"Something."

"What?"

Max-Ernest wrinkled his face. "Sebastian…"

Cass winced. "You mean his ashes?"

"Unless they were just cleaning out the fireplace…"

Cass stared at the jar. "They must be taking him on the cruise."

"The Egyptians mummified their pets all the time – it's kind of the same thing," said Max-Ernest. "I'll bet there'll be some cat mummies at the museum tomorrow. Hey, is that the trunk?"

The Jester's trunk was lying in the shadows beneath the tailgate. Cass had resisted crying ever since they'd arrived at the garage sale, but at the sight of the trunk her eyes welled with tears.

"What's wrong?" asked Max-Ernest. "Aren't you glad we found it?"

"It's Sebastian. He always helped us find everything. And now look, even when he's dead, he still is."

Cass laughed – and wiped her eyes with her sleeve.

★   ★   ★

The trunk was much too heavy for the two of them to carry all the way to Cass's house. They decided they would get their friend Yo-Yoji to help them move it later that evening. In the meantime, they pushed-pulled-heaved-shoved-lifted-dropped it into the small cement yard behind the firehouse.

"Hopefully, it'll be safe for a few hours," said Cass, standing victoriously over the trunk, her face pink and sweaty. "My grandfathers hardly ever come back here – as you can tell." She gestured to the long vines hanging from the firefighters' old basketball hoop.

"Aren't you gonna open it?" Distressed, Max-Ernest put his hand on the trunk. The layers upon layers of travel stickers and receipts and address changes formed a crust over the surface that made the trunk slightly forbidding but all the more tempting. He couldn't believe he'd put in all that effort and wasn't going to be rewarded with a peek. "For all we know, this is our only chance. When we come back, it'll be dark. And then—"

"Okay, okay," said Cass, who in truth wanted to look inside the trunk as much as Max-Ernest did. "Just don't ask any questions about…you know. I shouldn't have said anything about it."

"Then how'm I supposed to help?"

"You're not! That's what I'm trying to tell you."

"Okay, but just let me ask you one question," said Max-Ernest. "I was thinking about the story of the doctor who discovered the...it. Remember? The pharaoh executed him – after he told the pharaoh about the you-know-what."

Cass gave him a look that said, *Yes, I remember, but no, I don't want to talk about it.*

"He's the one who wrote on the papyrus, right?"

Cass nodded almost imperceptibly.

"Do you think the papyrus was stolen from his grave? It must have been, right? I mean, how else—?"

Cass glared at him. "Max-Ernest! Do you want me to open the trunk or not?"

"Yeah, yeah, okay."

Equally impressed and dismayed, Max-Ernest watched Cass work the large and complex combination lock that had stymied him months earlier when they first tried to open the trunk.

When she raised the trunk's lid, Max-Ernest gasped involuntarily.

Cass hadn't been exaggerating. *Treasure* was the right word. Inside the trunk, coins and jewellery and other precious objects sparkled tantalizingly – seemingly as bright and shiny as the day the lid first closed on them.

"Wow, your great-great-great-whatever-grandmother must have been a pretty good thief."

"Yeah, she was," said Cass proudly. "But she gave most of her stuff to the poor. I keep thinking – there must have been a reason she and the Jester left all this for me."

Cass started pulling things out for inspection. Max-Ernest regarded the objects with awe, almost afraid to touch them.

"At first I was going to donate it – you know, for disaster preparedness or to fight global warming or child slavery," she said, peering into a gold candlestick to see if anything was hidden inside. "But then I thought, who's going to believe it's mine?"

Cass opened a small silver box and found that it was full of uncut gems. They were beautiful even in their raw state and no doubt very precious, but they didn't provide what she really was hoping for: another clue about the Secret.

Max-Ernest turned his attention to the brass lock. He still couldn't get over the fact that Cass had managed to open it without him. He, not Cass, was supposed to be the expert combination cracker. Was she capable of finding the Secret without him, too? Of course, he wanted her to learn the Secret; so much depended on it. And yet—

"Hey, did you see this before?" he asked, examining the back of the lock. It protruded deeper into the trunk than might have been expected – like a box stuck to the inside of the trunk.

"Why?"

"Well, I was wondering why the back of the lock was so big – and then I saw this groove here, and I'm thinking that it might..."

He gripped the back of the lock and twisted; it unscrewed like the top of a jar.

"...come off like this," he said, now holding it in his hand.

The back of the lock turned out to be a small box lined with cracked, papery old leather. Inside was a gleaming gold ring tied to a strip of shredded linen.

"Look – I think it's Egyptian!" said Max-Ernest. "You think it belonged to the doctor?"

"Give that to me," said Cass quickly.

Max-Ernest reluctantly handed her the ring.

Unexpectedly heavy for its size, it was moulded from solid gold and resembled a signet ring. On top was a flat gold oval inlaid with lapis lazuli, the brilliant blue stone favoured by the ancient Egyptians. Some of the stone had been chipped away, but enough was left to show the original image: a long-beaked bird presented in profile in the classic Egyptian style.

When Cass saw the bird, her pointy ears tingled with excitement. "Hey, um, is there a hieroglyph that looks like this?"

"Why? Does it look like one of the hieroglyphs you saw?" Max-Ernest knew that the Secret was supposed to be Cass's, and Cass's alone – they had been warned repeatedly that it was dangerous for anyone else to share knowledge of the Secret – but it was impossible not to ask.

"Just answer the question."

"I thought you didn't want any help."

Cass gave him a look.

"Yeah, it's the hieroglyph of an ibis. The ibis was worshipped by the Egyptians, so you see a lot of them," said Max-Ernest, studying Cass's reaction. "But it isn't always just an ibis. Sometimes it's a symbol for Thoth—"

Cass tried to keep her facial expression neutral. "Thoth?"

"Remember from the spa? The god of magic and writing and judge of the dead?" (Years before, near the beginning of their adventures together, the god's name had proved vital in their quest to save Benjamin Blake at the Midnight Sun Spa.) "If you think about it, that would make more sense than an ibis. The Sec – I mean, *it* is supposed to be about immortality, right?"

"Max-Ernest! Thanks, but that's enough, okay?"

His mouth tightly closed, Max-Ernest contemplated this unwanted and unexpected shift in his relationship with Cass. In the past, the quest for the Secret had always brought the two of them together. Would it ever be that way again, he wondered, or would the Secret forever come between them?

Avoiding his glance, Cass examined the ring.

After the papyrus had turned to dust, Cass had the presence of mind to sketch the hieroglyphs in her notebook – but her memory was hazy, and her knowledge of hieroglyphs was scant. At best, the hieroglyphs she'd drawn bore a shaky resemblance to the originals.

During her studies for the Egypt unit, she compared her drawings over and over again to the hieroglyphs she'd seen – but with little luck. Before today, she'd succeeded in identifying only the first two of the five hieroglyphs: they meant *because* and *what*. Or she thought they did.

Now, thanks to the gold ring, she realized that the third hieroglyph depicted an ibis. She recognized the long curving beak. The rest of the bird – a football-shaped body atop stick-like legs – had been too smudged to read, at least in her recollection.

It wasn't much, and it didn't yet make any sense, but it was the beginning of the Secret:

Because what ibis

Or perhaps:

Because what Thoth

Mummies,
Middle School,
and Me

GRADUATION SPEECH

First Rough Draft (Or is it rough first draft? Or first draft of rough draft? Or...you get the point.)

By Max-Ernest, aka ME, i.e., Me, Myself, and I

ASSIGNED TOPIC: The Secret of Success

TITLE: Mummies, Middle School, and Me (That's alliteration, if you didn't know. Of course I know! I wrote it, duh... Wait, you did? Then who am I?)

Open with mummy joke:

Maybe —

What is a mummy's favourite musical programme? *Name That Tomb.*

— or —

What do you call a mummy who wins the lottery? A lucky stiff.

— or —

What did the sign at the Egyptian funeral home say?

SATISFACTION GUARANTEED OR DOUBLE YOUR MUMMY BACK.

(Question: do I have to credit book I get joke from?)

Transition:

All joking aside, you might think mummies are a funny thing to talk about in a graduation speech.

Thesis:

If you really think about it, however, graduation resembles mummification in many ways. Both involve preparing for the next stage of life — or, in the case of mummies, the afterlife.

(Nice one, Max-Ernest. *Blushes* Why, thank you, Max-Ernest. Don't mention it, Max-Ernest.)

Main Body of Speech (Ha-ha, get it? A mummy is a body — well, a dead one...):

As most people know, the mummification process begins with a corpse's brain being pulled out of his nose.

This is a lot like learning — only in reverse. In school, our teachers put things in our brains so every student "knows" (*knows/nose*, get it?) everything he should. Although, to be honest, I think some teachers pull stuff out of our brains and try to make us empty "airheads". (Probably shouldn't put that in this speech, should I?)

Semi-random factoid: the Egyptians thought people thought with their hearts, not their brains, so you'd have to say "airheart" if you wanted to insult their intelligence — not that you would. The Egyptians were pretty smart.

Anyway, the Egyptians wanted to take everything they could with them into the afterlife: servants, animals, food. But when you graduate, you can't necessarily take everything with you. Friends, for example. Everybody says that in upper school, sometimes people don't even talk to their old friends. It's like they don't exist...

Wait. Scratch that. What does that have to do with anything? Back to mummies—

CHAPTER
FIVE

A Field Trip

Max-Ernest had spent the entire bus ride to the Natural History Museum trying out mummy jokes for his graduation speech. (The opportunity to make a speech was an honour bestowed on him as Bookworm of the Year, winner of the Book-a-Day Reading Challenge; also, there was the fact that nobody else had volunteered.) By the time they neared their destination, his friends were brainstorming ways to silence him.

"Maybe we'll find some loose mummy bandages and we can gag him with them," suggested Yo-Yoji, who, as usual, had an entire seat to himself and was comfortably reclining with his long legs up, showing off his neon-orange sneakers.

Cass, sitting with Max-Ernest in the seat opposite Yo-Yoji, shook her head. "Nah, he would just tell jokes with his hands. Don't forget he knows sign language."

Max-Ernest nodded cheerfully. *How many mummies does it take to change a light bulb?* he signed, mouthing the words.

"Okay, so we tie his wrists together—" said Yo-Yoji, ignoring him.

"Forget it," said Cass. "He'll just tap Morse code with his foot."

Max-Ernest started tapping the floor: *N-O-N-E, T-H-E-Y L-I-V-E I-N E-T-E-R-N-A-L D-A-R-K-N-E-S-S.*

"Then we'll bury him in a sarcophagus," Yo-Yoji persisted.

Cass shook her head again. "With our luck, an earthquake will push it to the surface, and he'll jump out and tell some dumb joke about zombies—"

"Like this one?" asked Max-Ernest, grinning. *"Do zombies eat hamburgers with their fingers?"*

"See what I mean?"

"No, they eat their fingers separately!"

The plump boy who called himself Glob leaned over the seat in front of Max-Ernest. "Dude, zombies tell better jokes than you do – and I bet they give better graduation speeches, too."

"Leave him alone, man," said the boy sitting next to Glob, his voice muffled by the dreadlocks that covered his face. This was Daniel – more popularly known as Daniel-not-Danielle. "Zombies are cool. They kick mummy butt."

"They're not mutually exclusive categories, you know," said Max-Ernest. "Zombie equals dead body that comes back to life. Mummy equals dead body. Ergo, mummy that comes back to life equals—"

"Silence, please!"

It was Mrs. Johnson, standing up near the front of the bus.

Our friends shrank in their seats. Although they

were no longer quite as scared of their principal as they once had been, she still held the power to suspend them or even to prevent them from graduating middle school. And as much as they all feared graduating, there was one thing they all feared more: *not* graduating.

"Thank you," said Mrs. Johnson, holding onto her turquoise-blue hat as the bus lurched to a stop in front of the old brick museum. "Let's start practising our museum voices now. Remember, a museum is not a zoo. It is a place of quiet contemplation and reflection—"

UNWRAPPED: REAL MUMMIES!
DUSTY TOMBS. ANCIENT CURSES.
WALKING DEAD.

From King Tut to Boris Karloff*, mummies have long captured our imagination. Yet they are not

---

*BORIS KARLOFF WAS AN ACTOR WHO BECAME FAMOUS IN THE 1930S PLAYING DEAD BODIES THAT COME BACK TO LIFE. IF YOU ARE UNFAMILIAR WITH HIS OEUVRE, I HIGHLY RECOMMEND THE CLASSIC HORROR FILMS *FRANKENSTEIN* AND *THE MUMMY*. (IF YOU ARE UNFAMILIAR WITH THE WORD *OEUVRE*, IT IS THE BODY OF WORK OF AN ARTIST, WRITER, OR COMPOSER – LIVING, DEAD, OR OTHERWISE.) IN *THE MUMMY*, KARLOFF PLAYS IMHOTEP, A MUMMY REAWAKENED WHEN AN ARCHAEOLOGIST ACCIDENTALLY READS AN ANCIENT EGYPTIAN SPELL. BY FAR KARLOFF'S SCARIEST ROLE, HOWEVER, WAS SANTA CLAUS. HE DRESSED AS THE RED-SUITED HOUSEBREAKER EVERY CHRISTMAS AND HANDED OUT PRESENTS TO NEEDY CHILDREN, DOUBTLESS TERRIFYING THEM HALF TO DEATH.

just creatures of fantasy, haunting us on late-night television and on the streets at Halloween. They are material specimens of lost worlds – real people of the past whose bodies have been preserved so that we may study them today. What were their lives like? How did they die? What secrets do they hold in their ancient hands? Join us as these voyagers from the past take us on a journey across time.

SPECIAL THANKS TO EGYPT'S SUPREME COUNCIL OF ANTIQUITIES

EXHIBITION MADE POSSIBLE BY A GENEROUS GRANT FROM

SOLAR-ZERO LLC

Contrary to Mrs. Johnson's assertion, the museum was quite loud. The marble floors and vaulted ceilings magnified the kids' every footstep, and a lot of other sounds besides.

Most of the museum would be closed to the public for another two hours, and museum staff were using the time to repair exhibits and take inventory. It can be startling to hear soft-spoken curators shouting instructions or grave-faced museum guards joking with each other, but it certainly makes a museum livelier. If you've never visited a museum when it is closed, I recommend it; that's when a museum really comes to life.

The special, behind-the-scenes tour had been arranged by Daniel-not-Danielle's father, Dr. Albert Ndefo, who happened to be the chief curator of the mummy exhibit. Dr. Ndefo – also known as Albert 3-D, in reference to his three degrees: one in archaeology, one in anthropology, and one in Egyptology – greeted them next to the two-and-a-half-metre-tall stone sarcophagus that stood just inside the entrance, dwarfing anyone who passed by. "Hi, everybody, welcome to chaos. We're just doing a little rearranging before the noon rush!"

The Nigerian-born professor had dreadlocks like his son's, but at the moment his were tied back under an old, camouflage-patterned sun hat that looked as though it had been to the desert and back more than once. He wore a T-shirt that said ARCHAEOLOGY – DIG IT!, and he ushered his guests into the exhibit as if they were entering an excavation of buried ruins.

"Watch your backs," he warned. "The mummies most likely won't attack, but museum workers have been known to shoot poison darts."

As if on cue, a student bumped into a ladder, and a loose power cable fell down. Mrs. Johnson shrieked. Her students giggled.

"So, what is a mummy?" Albert 3-D asked

rhetorically, beckoning the last few stragglers inside. "Simple: a mummy is any dead body whose tissue has been preserved beyond the usual time. In this exhibit, we have naturally occurring mummies as well as man-made ones. Mummies created in caves, in sand, in icebergs – and even, in the case of bog mummies, *underwater*.* There are specimens from Peru, Chile, Greenland, Norway, and, of course, ancient Egypt. And then there are the animal mummies..."

The first room of the exhibit was large and grey, with few doors and fewer windows. It looked not unlike a tomb – a strange, futuristic tomb in which mummies were confined in protective glass cases. On the walls were big backlit photos of archaeological digs and ancient burial grounds that cast a ghostly fluorescent glow on the faces of the students.

The students fell silent as they got their first look at the mummies on display. While the bog mummies were hardly more substantial than rags, others looked strong enough to stand. Some were wrapped in the familiar linen bandages; others, in sheets. Some were naked; others were wearing elaborate jewelled garments. Some had hair; some were bald. Some were

---

*BOG MUMMIES, IF YOU'RE CURIOUS (AND I CAN'T IMAGINE THAT YOU AREN'T), ARE USUALLY FOUND IN THE BOGS OF NORTHERN EUROPE. THE PEAT IN THE BOGS ACTS AS A UNIQUE PRESERVATIVE – AND LEAVES THE FACES OF BOG MUMMIES UNIQUELY LIFELIKE.

sitting up; some, lying down. One was curled in a ball; another was slumped over.

A few students had to look away and take deep breaths; the mummies of **UNWRAPPED: REAL MUMMIES!** were altogether more real than they had imagined.

Yo-Yoji shook his head. "Ridiculous, man."

Max-Ernest nodded uncertainly. *Ridiculous* was a word that Yo-Yoji had been using often lately, but as with many of the words he adopted, you didn't always know if it was meant in a positive or negative sense – or in some other sense comprehensible only to those fluent in the language of cool.

"I'll let you look around, and then we'll talk in a few minutes," said Albert 3-D. "Unless someone has a question right now?"

"I do," said Glob. "Is it true people fart after they die? And if a mummy farts, will it still stink a thousand years later when his coffin is opened?"

His classmates tittered.

"Hmm...I doubt it," Albert 3-D answered seriously. "The smell would dissipate long before then. But you're right about dead bodies. In Mayan mythology, the god of the underworld was called Cizin, meaning *stinking one*."

*   *   *

While the rest of her class laughed, Cass slipped the ibis ring onto her finger.

It was a bit foolish of her to wear the ring in public, she knew, but holding a little piece of ancient Egypt in her hand gave her a sense of confidence. Maybe seeing the ibis next to other hieroglyphs in the exhibit would jog her memory; today, she was determined to identify the remaining hieroglyphs of the Secret.

Her backpack, as usual, had everything she might need:

Magnifying glass: check.

Hidden camera: check.

Moulding wax for taking impressions: check.

Brush for dusting specimens: check.

Armed like an archaeologist in the field, Cass looked in every place she might conceivably find a hieroglyph. While the other students casually checked out the exhibit, she methodically studied photos of tomb paintings and copies of spells from the *Book of the Dead.** She examined the decorations on funeral masks, and the carvings on stone sarcophagi. She

---

*THE EGYPTIAN *BOOK OF THE DEAD*, ALSO KNOWN AS THE *PAPYRUS OF ANI*, IS THE ESSENTIAL FUNERARY GUIDE THAT NO SELF-RESPECTING AMATEUR EGYPTOLOGIST CAN DO WITHOUT. TO QUOTE NO LESS AN AUTHORITY THAN ONE PSEUDONYMOUS BOSCH (SEE THE SECRET SERIES, BOOK 1), "IT INCLUDES MANY IMPORTANT SPELLS AND INSTRUCTIONS FOR SUCCESS IN THE AFTERLIFE – A USEFUL INTRODUCTION TO ANCIENT EGYPTIAN LIFE ABOVEGROUND AS WELL!"

inspected tiny *shabti* figures who were supposed to serve Egyptian nobles in the afterlife, and strange finger-shaped amulets meant to seal wounds and protect the dead.

And yet as far as she could tell, none of the hieroglyphs she saw resembled the hieroglyphs of the Secret. Then again, perhaps the sketches in her notebook were incorrect. There was no way to know.

Her confidence beginning to crumble, she stood, holding her notebook open in her hand and staring at a bowl of natron, the natural salt that is found in desert lakes and that was used by the Egyptians to dry out bodies before they were mummified. Could you mummify a body using normal table salt? she wondered idly. Maybe she should try it on herself. If she didn't figure out the Secret soon, she might as well be mummified.

As she turned away, Max-Ernest crept up behind her. He reached around and tapped her on her far shoulder –

She spun around, snapping her notebook shut. "What? Oh!"

She rolled her eyes when she saw Max-Ernest standing there, grinning at his little practical joke. "That is so not funny."

"Did you see the ibis mummies?"*

"Uh-huh."

Max-Ernest eyed the notebook in her hand. "Is that where you have your notes about...it?"

"Shh!" Cass whispered sharply.

"If you're so worried about people knowing, are you sure you should be wearing that ring?" asked Max-Ernest, stung.

Cass's ears flared red. "Why don't you go think of more jokes for your graduation speech or something?"

Max-Ernest watched her in consternation as she moved on to another display: **HAVE YOU EVER WONDERED WHAT A MUMMY'S SKIN FEELS LIKE? TOUCH HERE TO FIND OUT!** It was an interactive wall display containing swatches of leather, plastic, and other materials. She touched a few of the swatches and made a face.

"What's up with her?" asked Yo-Yoji.

Max-Ernest shrugged. "You know Cass."

---

*You may be interested to learn that ibis mummies are quite common. In the necropolis of Saqqâra – the Egyptians' famed City of the Dead – archaeologists discovered the mummies of one and a half million ibises. It is believed that the ibises were raised on farms specifically for the purpose of being mummified and offered to the gods. Upsetting? Perhaps. But consider the fate of a chicken.

Although Yo-Yoji was a fellow Terces member, it was Cass's business to tell him – or not – about the latest development in her search for the Secret. And truth be told, Max-Ernest didn't want to talk much about it. He was beginning to wish she'd never found the papyrus in the first place.

Yo-Yoji squinted. "Is that a ring on her finger? I've never seen her wear a ring before..." He looked askance at Max-Ernest. "You didn't give it to her, did you?"

"What? *No!* Why, were you planning on asking her to marry you?" asked Max-Ernest, recovering.

"Very funny..."

Yo-Yoji glanced at Cass again. It was almost as if he didn't like the idea of somebody else giving her a ring.

CHAPTER SIX

The Mystery Mummy

A moment later, Albert 3-D gathered all the students together and led the class towards a four-sided glass chamber that stood in the centre of the exhibit's largest room.

"Here is our star attraction," he said, opening the door to the chamber. "We keep the door closed during museum hours – you're supposed to look in from the outside – but since the public's not here yet, I thought I'd give you a treat."

Inside the chamber, a stone sarcophagus lay open for viewing. Next to it were three colourfully decorated wooden coffins that descended in size like Russian nesting dolls, and four clay canopic jars, each about the size of a paint can.* Like many jars of this kind, these ones were topped with the heads of a person, a falcon, a baboon and a jackal (who were supposed to guard the mummy's liver, intestines, lungs and stomach, respectively).

"Please, please, don't touch anything. Despite the fact that his grave was robbed repeatedly, this handsome fellow is one of the best-preserved mummies ever unearthed. His tomb was excavated just a year ago, and it's the first time the Egyptians have allowed him to travel."

---

*A CANOPIC JAR, AS YOU NO DOUBT REMEMBER FROM YOUR OWN STUDIES, IS A JAR IN WHICH THE ANCIENT EGYPTIANS STORED AND PRESERVED THE ORGANS OF THE DEAD.

Everyone gathered around the sarcophagus and eagerly stared down at the perfectly desiccated citizen of ancient Egypt.

"He's something of a mystery mummy. We don't even know his name. Around the museum, we call him Amun, which means *the hidden one*."

Tightly wound linen bandages surrounded most of the mystery mummy's body, but his head was bare, and his hands stuck out of the bandages just above his waist. His hair, assuming he'd ever had any, was long gone, and his skin had turned the colour of bronze sculpture. His eyes were closed, but his mouth was open, revealing a few rotten teeth and a dark hole where his tongue should have been.

"He looks like that painting they make Halloween masks out of," said Yo-Yoji. "What's it called?"

"*The Scream*," Max-Ernest volunteered.* "Maybe he was screaming in pain when he died. Then his mouth stayed open when rigor mortis set in. How 'bout that?"

"People scream for other reasons," said Cass. "He

---

*MAX-ERNEST MUST HAVE BEEN VERY PREOCCUPIED WITH THE MUMMY IN FRONT OF HIM. OTHERWISE, HE WOULD HAVE MENTIONED THAT THERE IS NOT JUST ONE PAINTING CALLED *THE SCREAM*; THERE ARE SEVERAL. THE ARTIST, EDVARD MUNCH, PAINTED THE SAME IMAGE MANY TIMES, AS IF HE COULD NEVER QUITE GET IT RIGHT. THE MESSAGE IS CLEAR: IF AT FIRST YOU DON'T SUCCEED...SCREAM. AND SCREAM AGAIN.

could have been trying to warn somebody about something. Like a sandstorm or a plague of locusts—"

"I think he looks like he's laughing," said Glob.

"Actually, none of you are right," said Albert 3-D. "His mouth was opened after his death. The Egyptians opened the mouths of mummies so they could breathe in the afterlife."

"So how did he die, then?" asked Cass.

"All we know about Amun is that he was a young doctor who rose to become the pharaoh's personal physician and adviser," said Albert 3-D. "Then, suddenly..."

He ran his finger across his neck – the universal sign for execution.

He pointed to the smallest of Dr. Amun's coffins, where some hieroglyphs were painted in black and red beneath the stylized face of a handsome young man.

"Daniel, do you want to read these glyphs for your classmates?" he asked, looking expectantly at his son.

Daniel-not-Danielle, who had remained remarkably quiet ever since they entered the museum, shook his head. His dreadlocks swung back and forth like a spinning mop.

"I'll read them," said Max-Ernest.

Albert looked at him in surprise. "You read hieroglyphs? Your Egypt unit was more in-depth than I thought."

Max-Ernest shrugged. "It's kind of a hobby."

"Some people collect trading cards or play video games." Glob snickered. "Max-Ernest reads hieroglyphs."

"I do those things, too!" Max-Ernest protested.

"He was being sarcastic," said Cass. "Just read it."

She looked over his shoulder, hoping that she might recognize one of her unidentified hieroglyphs. No luck.

Max-Ernest coughed exaggeratedly. "Ahem. Okay, here goes – 'The name of this man is…secret'? Is that the word?"

Albert 3-D nodded. "Go on."

"'Also secret is the reason for…'"

Max-Ernest stammered because a wild idea had just occurred to him. Could Dr. Amun be the doctor who had discovered the Secret? No, he thought, there's no way.

"'…for his death,'" read Albert 3-D, finishing the sentence. "That was very good. Have you considered going into Egyptology?"

"Yeah, I've considered it. But I still want to be a comedian. Or a comic magician." (Max-Ernest had a pretty good idea he was going to wind up being a writer instead, but he hadn't fully accepted it yet.)

"So nobody knows why Amun was executed?" asked Cass, who'd had the exact same idea about the mummy that Max-Ernest had had. (Only she didn't think the idea was so wild.)

Albert 3-D shook his head. "The inscription continues: 'Pharaoh asked for his wisdom, but he gave pharaoh only his wit.' . . . It sounds as though he made some kind of smart remark at the pharaoh's expense – the kind of thing one of you guys might say about, oh, a teacher or a principal."

He grinned at Mrs. Johnson. She didn't grin back.

"Whatever he did, I doubt we would think he deserved to die for it."

"In mummy movies, it's always the ones who are wrongfully executed who come back to life," said Yo-Yoji.

"Yeah, we better watch out," said Glob. "Or we're all going to die from the mummy's curse!"*

Albert 3-D chuckled. "I think the people burying

---

*The idea of the mummy's curse became popular when several men involved in the discovery of King Tutankhamen's tomb died soon after his disinterment. Later, people speculated that three-thousand-year-old bacteria released from Tut's tomb might have been to blame, but frankly there is even less basis for that theory. I would go with the curse.

him were a little worried about that, too. At the very end of the inscription, it reads: 'In life he had the magic touch. Now may his hands lie still.' Guess they were afraid he might reach out and grab them…"

As Albert 3-D led the class out of the sealed glass room, Cass, Yo-Yoji and Max-Ernest leaned over the edge of the sarcophagus to examine the mummy more closely.

"So – do you think it's him?" Cass whispered excitedly after everybody else had left.

"Who?" asked Yo-Yoji.

"Who do you think? The doctor who discovered the…you know."

Yo-Yoji nodded. "Right! And he was killed right after he told it to the pharaoh. Or after he refused to tell him. Whatever. It's almost exactly the same story."

"I thought of that, too, but it would be a pretty huge coincidence," said Max-Ernest. "Of all the mummies in the world, for this one to be that one particular doctor, here in our town, in an exhibit organized by our friend's dad. I highly, highly, highly doubt that is the case."

"A lot of things seem *highly*, *highly*, *highly* coincidental," said Cass, irked. "That doesn't mean they're not true."

"Plus, the hieroglyphs only said that the reason he was killed was secret," Max-Ernest persisted stubbornly. "Not that the reason was *a* secret or *the* Secret." Actually, he remembered as he said this, in ancient Egyptian the words *a* and *the* weren't always used, so there was little difference. But he didn't correct himself; he didn't want to give Cass the satisfaction.

"Well, I say it's him," said Cass, leaning in even closer to the mummy.

She didn't know how she knew, but she knew.

She'd come to the museum hoping to translate the rest of the Secret, but instead she'd discovered something potentially much more significant: the man who had discovered the Secret and who, for that reason, had suffered a pharaoh's wrath.

It was *his* dying hand, she was certain, that had written the Secret on a piece of papyrus thousands of years ago. And it was the same hand – with its long, bony fingers – that held Cass's attention now. Though the mummy's wrists were bound to his waist, his fingers stretched upwards, as if the mummy were straining to break free of the linen bandages. As if he wanted to touch her. To grasp her.

Transfixed, she stared at the mummy's fingers. She and Max-Ernest had found the ibis ring tied to a piece of shredded linen just like the bandages that wrapped the mummy. Could the ring once have encircled one of the mummy's fingers? Albert 3-D had mentioned something about the mummy's tomb being robbed...

The fingers were dark and crooked, with broken fingernails the colour of wood. She didn't see any signs of scraping or stretching where a ring might have been pulled off, but she couldn't be certain the signs weren't there because – frustratingly – a few of the fingers of the mummy's left hand were blocked from view by a stray bandage. If only she could move the bandage aside for a second...

She glanced over her shoulder. Max-Ernest had turned away, and Yo-Yoji was about to walk out of the glass room.

Taking a breath, Cass leaned down and gently pulled the bandage away from the mummy's hand. Immediately, she noticed the index finger: below the knuckle was a faint but discernible ring where the mummy's skin had turned black. The black ring narrowed at the sides of the finger and widened on top into a black oval. It was the exact shape of the ibis ring—

"Cassandra! Max-Ernest! Yoji! Get away from there!" Mrs. Johnson's voice broke Cass's concentration. "What part of 'do not touch' do you not understand?"

Cass spun around, her arms flailing in her attempt to distance herself from the mummy.

Too late, she realized her sweatshirt sleeve had caught on something.

She heard a snap, like the sound of a twig breaking, and the next thing she knew, a slim, dark projectile was flying through the air.

It arced over Max-Ernest's head, and as they all watched open-mouthed, it landed

right in the palm of Yo-Yoji's

hand.

He stared at it as if he had caught a live grenade.

It was the mummy's finger.

Sherds Not Shards

Let me take a wild guess:

You have never broken the finger off a mummy. (Don't feel bad about it; there's still time.)

Second wild guess:

You have, however, broken *something* valuable – maybe more than one something? – in the past.

They say time heals all wounds, but as you know from experience, that isn't true. Certainly, time does not mend all broken pots. It especially doesn't mend priceless Ming dynasty bowls, but I won't bore you with that story right now. (I will tell you this: I wasn't the one who thought it was a good idea to rest a fragile Chinese antique on top of a box of Belgian chocolates. Enough said.)

To return to the subject at hand, as it were, a broken finger is one thing; a broken-off finger, another. And a finger broken off a three-thousand-year-old corpse is an altogether different kettle of, er, something or other.

Everybody had an opinion about what to do with the miserable miscreants who had maimed the museum's mystery mummy.*

Mrs. Johnson suggested reporting the young

---

*Speaking of criminal carelessness, I fear I may have just exceeded my allowable alliteration allotment... Oops. There I go again!

offenders to the police right away – and, for good measure, to the Egyptian authorities as well.

"Vandalism is like a cancer," she said. "It must be treated quickly and brutally, or it will spread. Today it's a mummy. Tomorrow they will be defacing the *Mona Lisa*."

The administrators of the museum, who did not look very kindly on the breaking of ancient artefacts lent to them by foreign countries, were inclined to let the principal decide her students' fates.

Thankfully, the exhibit's curator had a cooler head.

The mummy was a priceless treasure, true, he agreed. This was a terrible accident, yes. But it was an accident. And accidents happen. Even to mummies. Even to King Tut!*

As the person who'd let students into the mummy's chamber, he, Albert 3-D, took full responsibility for

---

*I BELIEVE THE LEARNED PROFESSOR HERE WAS REFERRING TO A PARTICULAR PRIVATE PART OF KING TUTANKHAMEN'S. (YOU CAN GUESS WHICH PART I MEAN.) APPARENTLY, THIS PART WAS INTACT AND FULLY ATTACHED WHEN HOWARD CARTER FIRST EXHUMED THE MUMMY OF THE YOUNG PHARAOH IN 1922. IN THE 1960S, IT WAS NOTICED THAT THE PART HAD MYSTERIOUSLY BROKEN OFF, AND FOR YEARS NOBODY KNEW WHERE IT HAD GONE. MORE RECENTLY, HOWEVER, A CT SCAN OF KING TUT REVEALED THAT THE ROYAL APPENDAGE HAD FALLEN INTO THE SAND BENEATH THE MUMMY AND HAD LAIN THERE QUIETLY FOR YEARS, AWAITING DISCOVERY.

the incident. He would deal with any problems on the Egyptian side, and he would also put his mind to ways in which the kids could remedy their misdeed.

"Calling the police would not be helpful," he concluded.

Reluctantly, Mrs. Johnson surrendered the young offenders to his control.

"But as far as I'm concerned, you're all on probation," said the principal to Cass, Max-Ernest and Yo-Yoji. "If you want to graduate from middle school, you will do exactly as this man says. Otherwise, you will find yourselves repeating a grade. And, worse, spending another year with me!"

Albert 3-D soon came up with a plan, and late the very next afternoon – which happened to be a Saturday afternoon – the three chastened friends found themselves returning to the museum for their first round of "archaeology boot camp", as the curator called it.

Their new home-away-from-home, the Restoration Room, looked like a combination art studio and science lab – and, in fact, that's exactly what it was. On one side were the art supplies: paints, pens and pencils; plasters, clays and waxes; rolls of fabric and paper; spools of thread and twine; scissors of every size; and more types of glues and mastics than you ever imagined could possibly exist. On the other side were burners and beakers; acids and solvents; scales and thermometers; and all sorts of other substances and instruments for measuring and determining the age and composition of ancient and not-so-ancient objects.

Left to their own devices, I'm sure our enterprising young heroes could have done any number of things with all the materials at hand, from painting a masterpiece to building a bomb. Unfortunately, Albert 3-D had other plans for them.

When the archaeologist greeted them, he was holding an ordinary shoebox in his hands as delicately and carefully as if it were a Fabergé egg. Indeed, the shoebox contained something extraordinarily fragile: the mummy's finger, lying on a bed of linen like a miniature mummy in a miniature sarcophagus.

"I want you all to see this so you understand the situation you've left us in," he began sternly, without saying hello. "If you thought we could simply sew the finger back on, you're wrong. There are many questions to think about: will the operation further damage the mummy? What type of thread should we use? Would it be better to glue the finger to the hand? Or should we leave the finger off to show how the body is affected by the passage of time?"

As for the shoebox sarcophagus, its purpose was to recreate the conditions of mummification. Until the museum conservators figured out whether and how to reattach the finger, they wanted to store it in such a way that it would be preserved exactly as if it were still entombed under the sands of Egypt.

"Are you ready for your assignment?" Albert 3-D asked, placing the shoebox on a high shelf, next to a few urns that were in the process of being reassembled.

His three nervous charges looked at the long table in the middle of the room. It was covered with hundreds, perhaps thousands, of broken pieces of pottery.

"We're not supposed to organize *all* of those pottery shards, are we?" asked Max-Ernest.

"In archaeology, we call them *sherds*, not *shards*," said Albert 3-D. "And, yes, I want you to sort them all."

"That's what I meant – sherds," said Max-Ernest, embarrassed to be caught in such an obvious mistake (a mistake I'm sure *you* would never make).

The ceramic sherds-not-shards had been excavated from Dr. Amun's tomb and had been brought from

Egypt to make use of the museum's new magnetic-imaging equipment. The three friends' job: to sit on stools and separate the sherds-not-shards into piles by size and colour – and by nothing else.

"You might find some funny drawings on some of the sherds. The Egyptians liked cartoons, and a large number were found in Dr. Amun's tomb. But please ignore them," Albert 3-D warned. "Don't try to put the pieces back together – you'll just mess up everything."

With those encouraging words, Albert 3-D plonked himself down on the other side of the room to do some paperwork and let his prisoners get to work.

Their task turned out to be not unlike the early, sorting stage of a jigsaw puzzle – the main difference being that they were never supposed to go beyond that stage. Not surprisingly, this limitation proved extremely frustrating for Max-Ernest, who was expert at jigsaw puzzles, and for Cass, whose nature demanded that she investigate any mystery put in front of her. As for Yo-Yoji, he didn't like limits in general. Still, they were terrified of not graduating and didn't want to get into any further trouble, so they tried to do as they were told.

Albert 3-D hadn't said anything about talking, however.

"Yo, anybody else check Glob's blog last night?" asked Yo-Yoji.

The others shook their heads.

"So you don't know what happened to Amber, then?"

"Should I care?" asked Cass as she examined a sherd decorated with a bird painted in black. Could that be an ibis? she wondered, before putting it off to the side.

"Haven't you noticed that she's been gone for a week?"

"No. Why, did you miss her?" Cass teased.

"No!" Yo-Yoji glared.

Max-Ernest held up a sherd with the image of a scarab. "Hey, did you guys know a scarab was the same thing as a dung beetle?"

"Awesome," said Yo-Yoji. "You guys want to hear about Amber or not?" He looked at them to make sure he had their full attention.

"Okay, what happened?" asked Max-Ernest.

"She went blind."

"Blind?!" the other two echoed in chorus.

"Well, sort of blind – she could still see light and stuff," Yo-Yoji amended, enjoying the effect his words were having. "And it was only for a day."

"Did she get a chemical burn? Or was it viral?" asked Cass, her mind racing through all the scenarios she'd studied.

Yo-Yoji shook his head. "Nothing like that. Glob said that Veronica said that Amber had some mystery disease or something – whatever it was, the next morning she woke up and she couldn't see a thing."

"That's awful," said Cass, although, as everybody knew, she had wished far worse on Amber in the past. "And I'll bet anything that she's never even done any sensory-deprivation training."

(Going blind was one of Cass's top ten fears – above malaria and below cerebral haemorrhage; she trained for it constantly.)

"Glob says it's a huge secret. 'Course, that didn't keep him from writing about it," Yo-Yoji snickered.

Albert 3-D looked up from his desk. "Why doesn't it sound like you guys are working?"

"Sorry!" they cried in unison.

After that, they were quiet – for at least three minutes.

Then Yo-Yoji broke the silence again: "Hey, is this one of those cartoons he was talking about?" He held up a largish sherd on which someone had drawn a mouse sitting on a throne. "The mouse is supposed to be a pharaoh, right?"

"Well, he's sitting on a throne and wearing a pharaoh's crown and beard, so, yeah, I would say so," said Max-Ernest.

"Okay, Mr. Knows-Everything-About-Shards, I mean sherds," said Yo-Yoji. "If it's so obvious, what's that coming out of his ear?"

"It's the beak of an ibis," said Cass. "Look."

Cass took Yo-Yoji's sherd from him and placed it next to the sherd she had put aside. "I noticed this one before..."

Reunited, the two pieces of pottery showed an ibis standing beside the mouse pharaoh's throne and whispering in his ear. The mouse was pounding on his sceptre, his whiskers twitching angrily – not a very flattering portrayal of a potentate.

Cass felt a familiar tingle in her ears. She had no doubt what the illustration meant. "So, do you guys *still* not think the mummy was him?" she whispered.

Before they could respond, Albert 3-D stood up, shaking his head. "You guys are hopeless. I can see why you're always getting in trouble with your principal." He smiled. "I like that about you."

Reminding them to focus on their work, he told them he would be leaving them alone for twenty minutes or so. The exhibit would be moving to the

Cairo Hotel in Las Vegas in a few days, and there were many details to arrange.

As soon as their not-so-strict-after-all chaperone had left, Yo-Yoji turned back to Cass. "So you think the ibis is the doctor who discovered the... it?"

Cass nodded. "Look, he's even whispering in the pharaoh's ear."

"And that means he's Dr. Amun, the mummy right here in this museum? Ridiculous!" said Yo-Yoji, amazed at the coincidence. "It's so ridiculous it's *re-sick-ulous*!"

"I told you – there was a mark from the ibis ring on the mummy's finger," said Cass, pulling the ibis ring out of her pocket to show Yo-Yoji. "It has to be him."

(On the way to the museum that afternoon, Cass had filled Yo-Yoji in on their findings about the ibis and the Secret.)

"Can I see?" Yo-Yoji, who'd never seen the ring up close before, reached for it – then jerked his hand back in surprise. "Whoa! Did you feel that shock?"

Cass nodded, rattled. "It's the ring. It... buzzes sometimes when you touch it. I don't know why."

Max-Ernest looked curiously at it. "That's strange. They definitely didn't have batteries in ancient Egypt."

"We can think about it later," said Cass, slipping the ring back into her pocket. "We don't have much time..."

"Uh, time for what?" asked Max-Ernest suspiciously.

"To go look at the mummy, of course," said Cass.

Max-Ernest looked at her in alarm. "Right now? The museum's closed."

"Yeah, it's perfect. Nobody's around to bother us. The exhibit is right upstairs."

"Cool," said Yo-Yoji, who was so antsy after forty-five minutes in the Restoration Room that he would have accepted any excuse to leave.

"Albert 3-D is going to come back any second," said Max-Ernest, aghast. "We're in enough trouble already!"

"I know, and I want to graduate as much as you do," said Cass. "But think about it: the papyrus and the ring, the only clues we have about the...thing, were both stolen from Amun's grave. Maybe there's something else in his sarcophagus, or wrapped up with him or something, that the tomb robbers didn't get."

"So now *you* want to go rob his grave?"

"No, just look at it!" said Cass, exasperated. "We'll never have a chance like this again."

"For all we know, it's totally dark up there," said Max-Ernest.

"Are you scared?" asked Yo-Yoji.

"Of what you guys will do, yes! Anyway, how do we know the alarm's not on?"

"They don't put the alarms on until later at night," said Cass. "Too many people are walking around before that."

"You asked?"

"I thought you wanted to help," said Cass, avoiding the question.

She pulled a small penlight out of her pocket, ready to go.

"Now I know for sure you planned this," said Max-Ernest.

"What do you mean?"

"The flashlight."

"I always carry a flashlight."

"Yeah, in your backpack. But that one is the extra one you only take when we're going on a mission."

"Fine, you busted me. Are you in or aren't you?"

Max-Ernest looked from Cass to Yo-Yoji and back again.

He was still sore at Cass. She seemed to want his help only when it was convenient for her. Otherwise, the Secret was hers alone to discover. And yet, if this truly was their one chance to discover it – *her* one chance to discover it, he corrected himself – he had no choice. He had to go along. In the end, the Secret was bigger than either of them.

"I'm in," he said.

A Scream in the Darkness

In order to get upstairs, they first had to walk through the Osteology and Taxidermy Room – in other words, the room in which the bones of a raptor would be reassembled, or a lifeless raccoon stuffed. Enough animal heads lined the walls to fill a dozen hunting lodges. In one corner, there were so many hair and whisker samples it could have been a hair salon for woodland animals. In another corner, carefully labelled little bones sat in boxes, like parts at a repair shop. Bigger bones lay in rows on tables, and three partly assembled dinosaur skeletons struck poses around the room.

Yo-Yoji picked up the femur of a large mammal off a table. "You think if I toss this, any of them will run after it?"

Like most museums, the Natural History Museum had many more items in storage than on display. After our friends left the Osteology and Taxidermy Room, they found themselves weaving through racks of Native American tribal garments and headdresses, bows and arrows and other assorted weapons, even a tepee hanging upside down from the ceiling. Next were the seal coats and harpoons of Eskimos, and a collection of pans and tools and other memorabilia from the gold rush, followed by a pair of nineteenth-century sea-diving suits that looked like antique astronauts.

After that, the collections became too eclectic to categorize. It's very likely that not even the curators of the museum knew everything they had.

An unmarked door opened into a stairwell that led to the museum upstairs. Quietly, they crept up the stairs, hoping nobody was waiting for them at the top.

"Aargh!" Cass spun around when she reached the landing above. "Max-Ernest, I'm going to kill you if you tap me like that one more time!" she said in an angry whisper.

From several metres behind, Max-Ernest looked at her in confusion. "What do you mean? I didn't!"

Yo-Yoji nodded. "I can back him up. Right there the whole time."

Cass's ears turned pink. "Oh. Sorry. I guess I'm just a little jumpy. Come on, let's go." She brushed past a potted palm and headed towards the mummy exhibit.

Just as Max-Ernest had feared, in contrast to the fluorescent-bright hallways below, the galleries upstairs were barely lit. Aside from a few dim lights here and there, the museum was dark. Not so dark you couldn't see your own hands. But too dark to read the labels on the displays, let alone to read hieroglyphs.

Cass turned on her flashlight. The beam landed on the bottom of the sign introducing the exhibit.

"Hey, did you guys see that before?" Max-Ernest asked, peering at the sign. "'Exhibition made possible by a generous grant from SOLAR-ZERO LLC.'"

"So?" asked Cass, impatient to get to the mummy.

"It's just a weird name, that's all. If they're a solar-power company, why *zero*?"

"Maybe they make sunglasses, like zero UVA rays?" suggested Yo-Yoji.

"All I know is my flashlight is solar, and it's going to lose its power in a minute."

Cass pushed ahead into the exhibit, her flashlight thrust forward as if she meant to ward off any attackers along with the darkness.

If you've ever explored a crypt in the middle of the night (and knowing you, you have), then I don't need to tell you how unnerving it is to see a flashlight beam land on the face of a corpse. Imagine, then, what a mummy might look like. Then multiply that by about fifty (the approximate number of mummies in the exhibit, including cats, dogs, birds and crocodiles). For all her bravery, Cass soon stopped waving the flashlight around and kept it pointed at the floor.

Ahead of them, in the centre of the gallery, Dr. Amun's glass chamber glinted forebodingly.

"What was that?" Cass whispered.

"What?" asked Max-Ernest.

"Didn't you hear footsteps?"

"I thought that was you."

"I thought it was a guard," said Yo-Yoji.

They all stood still for a moment. But there was no other sound.

Slowly, gingerly, they tiptoed towards the glass chamber.

The door was slightly ajar. Cass entered first, and by the time Max-Ernest and Yo-Yoji let themselves in, she was already standing over the sarcophagus.

Before they caught up with her, they heard something they'd rarely heard in all the dangerous and death-defying adventures they'd shared with Cass.

The sound of Cass screaming.

No, this isn't a new chapter, I'm just prolonging the...

s u s p e n s e.

I guess that's enough.

Well, maybe just one more...

m o m e n t.

Okay, here's what happens next:

With Cass's scream echoing in their ears, Max-Ernest and Yo-Yoji ran to where she was standing by the mystery mummy's open sarcophagus.

"What happened?" asked Yo-Yoji. "Are you all right?"

"No..." Cass looked unharmed, but she was breathing hard and clutching her stomach.

"Did something scare you?" asked Max-Ernest. "Was there a rat?"

"No, nothing like that," said Cass, her ears red with embarrassment. (She did not think of herself as the kind of girl who screamed in fright.) "I was just a little surprised, that's all. Look!"

Max-Ernest and Yo-Yoji looked down and saw –

Nothing.

All that was left in the sarcophagus was a little spider crawling across the sandy bottom. The mummy was gone.

CHAPTER
NINE

Bloody Fingers

By the time Cass closed the door to her bedroom, she hardly had any fingernails left. She'd chewed them down to the nubs. Two of her fingertips were bleeding, gruesome reminders of the ancient finger that had signalled the beginning of her latest troubles. Her fingers hurt, but she didn't mind the pain: she deserved it.

She'd never felt worse.

Never more guilty. She was the one who'd broken off the mummy's finger. She was the one who had encouraged her friends to sneak back into the exhibit, making it look as though they had stolen the mummy. She was the one who had betrayed the trust of Albert 3-D.

Never more anxious. She didn't know what punishment was in store for her friends and herself. Expulsion? Jail time? Whatever it was, not graduating from middle school was likely to be the least of it.

Never more afraid. Somebody had taken the mummy. Somebody who knew it was the mummy of the man who'd discovered the Secret. Somebody ruthless and disdainful of the consequences. Somebody who very likely knew about Cass and her friends as well.

Worst of all, she, Cass, was no closer to finding the Secret. With the mummy gone, she was further away from the Secret than ever.

As she sat down on her bed, she looked up at all the old photos and magazine articles that covered her walls. They depicted disaster and destruction of countless varieties. Floods. Fires. Earthquakes. Explosions. Storms. Plagues. Animal attacks. Heatwaves and droughts. Water and power shortages. War. Famine. Asteroid impacts. Meteorites. The list went on. But nothing that anticipated her current predicament.

She'd spent her whole life preparing for sudden, unexpected events over which she would have little or no control. And yet here she was, dealing with a calamity that was almost entirely of her own making.

Why did she have to break the mummy's finger? Why did she have to insist on going back upstairs? Why couldn't she ever leave well enough alone?

She, Cass, was the disaster. Instead of preparing for earthquakes, she thought, she should have been preparing for *herself*.

Her mother opened the door without knocking.

"Albert called," she said, looking not at Cass but at some invisible point in the distance. "He's very disappointed in you and your friends."

"No kidding."

"He wants to see us all first thing in the morning."

"What about school?"

"Tomorrow is Sunday."

"Oh yeah."

"Besides, you'll be lucky if you're allowed back to school."

"I told you we didn't—"

"Save it, Cassandra." Her mom slammed the door shut.

Cass stared at it. Her mother had said almost nothing all night – as if she had given up on Cass altogether. Cass would much have preferred a good fight. She knew her mother thought that she and her friends had taken the mummy. If her mother had come right out and said so, then Cass could have defended herself and had the pleasure of being angry at all the horribly unfair and totally unforgivable things her mother said. Her mother's silence was excruciating.

Fully dressed, Cass crawled under the covers, ready to abandon herself to tears and self-pity.

But she couldn't. It wasn't in her nature.

Unbidden, the image of Pietro, beloved leader of the Terces Society, entered her head. He always told her how much he believed in her, the Secret Keeper. She couldn't let him down. Not now.

Sit up, she told herself. You're a survivalist. Think like one.

What to do?

She pulled the ibis ring out of her pocket and put it on her finger, hoping it might supply an answer.

Just a short time earlier, the ring had made her feel so confident. Then there was the excitement of finding the mummy, the so-called Dr. Amun. For a moment, it had seemed like such a breakthrough. The man who had discovered the Secret – what could bring her closer to discovering the Secret herself? Now Amun was missing. And the ring was seeming more mysterious than helpful.

It buzzed almost uncomfortably, and she took it off. What made it do that? she wondered. Did the ring have a more definite power? A clearer purpose?

She inspected the ring for the tenth or twentieth time. There was no inscription on the inside of the band; it didn't say TO MUMMY WITH LOVE or UNTIL THE AFTERLIFE DO US PART or THANKS FOR THE MUMMERIES or anything like that, not even in hieroglyphs. The only hieroglyph on the ring was the ibis carved into the blue stone. At first Cass had wondered if maybe there was a secret compartment under the ibis, but the top of the ring didn't screw off and there didn't seem to be any latch or hinge.

Giving up on the ring inspection, she searched through her desk drawer and located a thin gold chain her grandfathers had given her as a birthday present a few years earlier. She'd never worn it before (as a rule, she considered necklaces worse than frivolous; they were a choking hazard), but now she threaded the chain through the ring and hung it around her neck.

Far from a good-luck charm, the ring was beginning to seem more like a talisman of doom, but she had a distinct feeling it was safest to keep the mysterious gold artefact near her at all times.

The Rabbit, the Cat and the Carrot:
A Look Behind the Scenes of the Secret Series

We are inside a small room strewn with books and chocolate bar wrappers – PB's office. A rabbit sits at a desk, typing furiously, while PB lies on a couch with his feet up. Next to PB, a cat lazily licks her paws.

PB: . . . and after Max-Ernest solved the hardest puzzle on earth and saved her life against all odds, Cass looked him in the eyes and said, quote, "Max-Ernest, you're a hero. And my best friend. And really funny. Forget everything I said. I apologize."

The sound of typing stops. Silence.

PB: Quiche, do you have that? "I apologize" – with a z.

Rabbit: Yeah, I got it.

PB *(sitting up)***:** But. . .?

Rabbit: But (a) it's not true. That girl never apologized for anything. And (b) the one who owes an apology is you. . .to me!

PB *(sighs)***:** Is this because I cut your carrot rations?

Rabbit: How would you like it if I stopped letting you eat chocolate?

PB: You were turning orange!

Rabbit: So? It's my favourite colour… Besides, how could any rabbit write with that thing licking licking licking all day?

Cat *(bristling)*: I am a cat and I have a name.

Rabbit: Oh, that's right, what is it? Cocoa?

PB and cat *(in unison)*: Cacao!

Rabbit: Of course, Cacao… Cacao…rhymes with "Meow, meow, gee, how I love the taste of my own fur!"

The cat arches her back and hisses, ready to spring. The rabbit's nose twitches nervously. Then the cat settles back down. She can't be bothered.

Cat *(to PB)*: Will you please give this bunny a carrot already?

PB: But I just gave him half my chocolate.

Rabbit: How many times do I have to tell you? RABBITS DON'T LIKE CHOCOLATE!

PB: Okay, okay, I just don't understand…

Rabbit: One word: Easter.

PB: Easter?

Rabbit: All those chocolate bunnies? Would you like to see yourself eaten in effigy every year by hordes of ravenous children?

PB: Fine, no chocolate. But, Quiche, I was on a

roll! If you want a carrot, start typing.

Rabbit: You call that a roll? I call it self-aggrandizing drivel. Why can't you write a real book, like—

Cat: Oh, here we go – *Watership Down* again! The only book he ever read all the way without chewing…

Rabbit: That's it. I'm leaving!

The rabbit hops off his chair…and jumps into a shiny top hat that's sitting on the floor. He disappears from sight.

Moments later…

Dangling a carrot from his hand, PB crouches by the top hat. The cat contentedly licks her paws.

PB: Here, bunny bunny bunny!

Cat: Trust me, that never works.

PB *(to hat)***:** Please, Quiche, I can't write this book without you!

Rabbit *(unseen, in hat)***:** Oh, so now he admits it!

PB: I'm begging you…

The rabbit peeks his nose out for a second, then disappears again.

Rabbit: Is that all I'm worth to you?

PB: Fine...

He holds out the entire bunch of carrots. A single rabbit paw emerges – just long enough to grab the bunch of carrots – then disappears back into the hat.

PB: Quiche! Aargh!

The sound of munching. Carrot greens and scraps fly out of the hat. The end of a carrot lands on the cat's nose. The cat lets out an exasperated sigh of disgust.

Rabbit *(inside hat, still munching)***:** And what if I couldn't type? Would you just let me rot in this hat for ever?

PB: That's not fair. You know I love you, little buddy. We've been through thick and thin together.

Rabbit *(belches)***:** Mostly thin. If you had it your way, I'd be starving.

PB: We'll both be starving if we don't get this book finished.

The rabbit finally sits up in the hat and rests his head on his paws.

Rabbit *(dreamily)***:** Remember when we were on the road? You and me and that pigeon you used to dust with baby powder so he looked like a dove?...

PB: Face it, Quiche. Magic isn't our thing. We weren't any good. They threw vegetables at us!

Rabbit: I know – I've never eaten so well.

PB: Can we please go back to writing?

Rabbit: You know why you're such a terrible magician? Because magicians aren't supposed to reveal their tricks. And you—

PB: Don't tell me: I can't keep a secret.

Cat *(from couch)*: Well, at least we all agree about something.

END

CHAPTER
TEN

A Thing

Daniel-not-Danielle had a very mixed reaction when he heard about the mummy being stolen. He knew he should be angry – it was his father's exhibit, after all – and yet, when he thought about it, he had to admit he wasn't angry at the thieves so much as jealous. He almost wished that he had been with them.

That *he* had stolen the mummy.

Not really, of course. He'd had enough of mummies to last a lifetime – and well into the afterlife. But maybe *that* was what was so thrilling about the thought of absconding with one.

Mummies weren't just his father's job; they were his father's hobby and, Daniel-not-Danielle sometimes felt, they were his father's family as well. His father collected what he called "mummy-abilia", and their apartment was full of modern-day archaeological artefacts like Halloween mummy costumes and candy Gummy Mummies; mummy key chains and coffee mugs and salt and pepper shakers; toy mummies that unravelled in long strips or glowed in the dark or even, in one case, walked and talked; posters of mummy movies and TV shows; and, most precious of all, mummy dummies and props.

His father's prized possession: a wax hand from the 1940 movie *The Mummy's Hand.* Once, when Daniel-not-Danielle was younger, he had made the mistake of taking it to school to scare his friends. It was the angriest he had ever seen his normally easy-going father.

Until now.

Today was Sunday, and they should have been having pancakes at the diner down the street, followed by a trip to the news-stand to look at comic books – their Sunday morning ritual for the last four years. (Pancakes and comic books were among the few things both he and his father liked, although Daniel-not-Danielle preferred blueberry pancakes, and his father the buckwheat variety; his father preferred DC Comics, and Daniel-not-Danielle the Marvel line-up.) There would be no pancakes this morning, however. Daniel-not-Danielle had to content himself with cold cereal.

His father had warned him not to eavesdrop on the meeting, but his father had also suggested he do his homework; and, as his father knew, Daniel-not-Danielle always did his homework at the kitchen table. Was it his fault that the kitchen was next to the living room and that he could hear every word said in the meeting, whether he was trying to or not? And if by chance he happened accidentally to peek through the keyhole in the door, and therefore he could see almost everything, too, well, how could he be blamed for that?

The living room was small and filled with Albert 3-D's mummy-abilia. Nobody looked comfortable. Max-Ernest was sitting on the couch, squeezed between his parents. His forehead was red and furrowed as if he were trying with all his might to keep his parents apart or maybe to pull them together – it was hard to tell which. Cass was pacing back and forth in front of her mother, who was sitting tensely in the rocking chair. Every time Cass passed by, the chair rocked and her mother grimaced with annoyance. Of all the people in the room, Yo-Yoji looked the most relaxed, leaning against the wall. But even his jaws tensed whenever his father or mother, standing huddled beside him, said something in his ear.

Daniel-not-Danielle's father, Albert 3-D, was sitting on his desk chair, wheeled in from his office. A bowl of Gummy Mummies lay untouched on the table.

"Let me ask you this," said Cass after the initial introductions had been made. "If we stole the mummy, where did we hide it? How could we get it out of the museum before the security guard found us? It's not like we put it in our pockets!"

Unable to see her face from his vantage point in the

kitchen, Daniel-not-Danielle nevertheless thought she sounded very adult and forceful. Score one for his friends.

"Besides, why would we even do it in the first place?" asked Yo-Yoji, jumping in. "You think we would steal something like that just for laughs? It's way too hairy. We don't want to go to jail!"

Good point, thought Daniel-not-Danielle. If it was just about a prank, why not put a pair of Groucho Marx glasses on a mummy? Or a Hawaiian shirt and flower lei, maybe. Stealing a mummy was pretty extreme.

"Actually, that's not really an argument in our defence," Max-Ernest cautioned. "There are lots of other reasons we might have done it besides laughs. People collect all kinds of things. Bugs. Bones. Stamps. A mummy would be priceless to some people. I know for certain that you could sell—"

Cass and Yo-Yoji glared at him. He trailed off.

Watching through the keyhole, Daniel-not-Danielle stifled a giggle. Max-Ernest never knew when not to talk.

All three of them had such distinct personalities, Daniel-not-Danielle reflected. They all had their *things*. Max-Ernest: hyper-talkative, relentlessly going on about jokes and magic. Cass: a "survivalist", or whatever it was she called herself. Yo-Yoji: the cool guy with the sneaker collection, the guitarist.

He, Daniel-not-Danielle, didn't have a thing. Comic books didn't count; almost everybody liked them. His closest thing to a thing was his hair. But his dreadlocks didn't signify anything about his personality; it was just hair. Besides, his father had dreadlocks, too. Sometimes, Daniel-not-Danielle felt as if he were one of a group of superheroes, each with a unique super-power – except for him. The guy who had no *thing*.

Maybe that was part of it. Stealing a mummy – that would have been a thing. Certainly, it was a crazy enough caper to be worthy of a comic book. On the other hand, mummy stealing – who would want *that* to be their thing? In stories and movies about mummies, tomb robbers were always portrayed as snivelling, sneaky creatures, no better than rats. Daniel-not-Danielle certainly didn't want to be one of them.

"Hold on, guys – let's talk this through slowly," said Albert 3-D. He looked haggard. As Daniel-not-Danielle knew, his father had been up all night – puttering, pacing, swearing – handling the fallout from the theft. "This is a very big deal. There could be an international scandal – we're going to have to alert the Egyptian Embassy. The museum director wanted to give the police your names, but I begged him to wait until I spoke to you again. That's why you're here – I'm hoping you can shed some kind of light on what happened."

As Albert 3-D laid it out, the case against his son's friends was very strong:

a) They had a history of vandalizing the mummy (whether intentionally or accidentally).

b) There was video footage of them entering the exhibit around the time the mummy was stolen.

c) Nobody else was seen entering the exhibit that night.

d) In addition, there was an eyewitness – a security guard – who had caught them lingering around the mummy's empty sarcophagus.

"Yeah, but did the guard see us take the mummy?" asked Yo-Yoji. "At any point in the video, did you actually see us take it?"

Albert 3-D shook his head.

"No, he didn't, because we didn't do it," said Cass. "We don't steal things!"

"That's not what your principal says," said Albert 3-D.

"Yeah, but that wasn't really stealing," said Max-Ernest. "She's just talking about the time we—"

His friends glared at him again. Max-Ernest switched course. "The point is – all the evidence is circumstantial. You said we were the only ones seen entering. Was anyone seen exiting? Maybe somebody could have come in when the museum was open, and they could have hidden in the room until after closing time – and then taken the mummy? How 'bout that?"

"The video is a little…inconclusive," Albert 3-D admitted. "Do you have any reason to believe somebody stayed? Did you see anybody? If you speak now, it will be better for all of us."

"Does that mean you saw somebody exiting with the mummy in the video?" asked Yo-Yoji.

"Not *with* the mummy, no," said Albert 3-D.

"But there was someone else?" Yo-Yoji insisted.

Albert 3-D hesitated. "I'm really not supposed to say—"

"So you think we're his accomplices?" asked Max-Ernest.

"That's one theory—"

"Can we see the video?" asked Cass.

"Sorry. I was very specifically instructed not to share it."

"That isn't fair," said Max-Ernest. "Without all the evidence, how can we mount our defence?"

"Now, slow down, son," said Max-Ernest's father. "If the museum doesn't press charges, the police can't investigate, isn't that right?"

"Don't get ahead of yourself, Max-Ernest," said Max-Ernest's mother. "The police can launch an investigation only if the museum presses charges, correct?"

"It makes no difference," said Albert 3-D, only slightly put off by the repetitive nature of the questions. (He had met Max-Ernest's parents before.) "If the museum doesn't press charges, the Egyptians probably will."

"So should we be hiring lawyers for our kids, Albert?" asked Yo-Yoji's father.

"It's not a bad idea."

"Nobody's pressing charges," said Cass's mother. "These kids will tell you everything. They'll get your mummy back for you, I promise."

"But, Mom, we don't know anything!" said Cass, outraged.

"Sweetheart, didn't you hear what he said? They looked at the video footage. If you didn't take it yourselves, you must know something."

"I can't believe you won't believe me – your own daughter! Why don't you ask Albert 3-D what he was doing when the mummy was stolen? He's the one who collects mummies."

"Cassandra!" Her mother glared at her.

"Well, it's true. Look around you. And he probably had more opportunity than anyone—"

"Cass, please be quiet before you make things much worse for yourself," said her mother. "Albert, you'll have to excuse my daughter. She's a little upset."

"I understand."

"Think about how a police record would affect these kids' futures. Can you just give us a little time?" Cass's mother looked hopefully at Albert 3-D.

"I'll try to hold off the dogs, but I can't promise," said Albert 3-D. "The exhibit is supposed to move to Las Vegas in three days. If the mummy doesn't turn up before then, I'm afraid the police are going to have more than a few questions."

After that, everybody spoke at once.

In the kitchen, Daniel-not-Danielle stewed. He had assumed his friends were guilty – there seemed to be no other explanation – but now he had his doubts.

Either they were innocent or they were better actors than he thought they were. Max-Ernest, especially.

Daniel-not-Danielle didn't think Max-Ernest could lie about something like this to save his life.

If they didn't do it, who did?

For a second, he wondered if Cass's wild accusation about his father could be right. But he could think of no real motive. Contrary to Cass's suggestion, the last thing his father would want to add to his collection was a real mummy. His father had more than enough of those at work.

While people continued to discuss the missing mummy in the living room, Daniel-not-Danielle came to a decision. As quietly as he could, he walked down the hallway to his father's home office. His father's desk was covered with books and journals and notepads, but he didn't have to look for very long: the security disc was right on top of a pile of magazines. He could tell what it was because the museum's name was on the label, along with the previous day's date.

Quickly, he inserted the disc into his father's computer and started to save the contents of the disc onto the hard drive. In a moment, he would condense the file and e-mail it to his friends.

The wax hand from *The Mummy's Hand* sat on a shelf right next to his father's desk, a silent witness to his little act of digital thievery. Daniel-not-Danielle gave the hand a good stare and defiantly stuck out his tongue. In his imagination, the hand responded with a wave of acquiescence. Copying the video was the most legally questionable thing Daniel-not-Danielle had ever done. And yet he almost thought his father would want him to do it.

It wasn't stealing a mummy. It wasn't even aiding and abetting the stealing of a mummy. In a way, it was the opposite, he thought as he pressed Send: he was helping his friends prove they hadn't stolen a mummy – perhaps even helping them solve the crime.

In comic books, it was usually the villains who pressed buttons – to set off bombs, for example. The heroes raced to stop them. Nonetheless, Daniel-not-Danielle felt, it was a start.

Daniel-not-Danielle: button pusher, crime fighter.

Maybe that would be his thing.

CHAPTER
ELEVEN

Video Stars

"**W**ho's there? Show me your hands!"

The security video ended there, with the nervous museum guard advancing on the three of them, his hand on his nightstick. In the centre of the frame was a frozen Max-Ernest, spooked by the appearance of the guard.

It was Sunday night and – thanks to Daniel-not-Danielle – Cass, Max-Ernest and Yo-Yoji had all been watching the video simultaneously on their computers at home, messaging each other at frequent intervals.

> **guitarsamurai:** dude, you look like you saw a ghost.
>
> **survivor3000:** he always looks like that, it's the hair.
>
> **juniorjester:** u guys going to make fun of me all night? thought we were trying to avoid getting arrested.
>
> **guitarsamurai:** just practising for juvenile hall. we're going to have to entertain ourselves there.
>
> **survivor3000:** okay, let's get serious. my mom's going to check on me any sec. I can feel it.

They knew what happened next, after the video ended: the guard's relief when he realized it was just the three kids Albert 3-D had introduced earlier. His scolding them for wandering around the gallery unsupervised. Then his shock when he discovered the mummy was missing. His insistence that they not move until the head of security arrived along with Albert 3-D.

Et cetera. Et cetera.

It was what happened earlier that they had questions about.

They decided to watch the video again from the beginning.

As Albert 3-D had said, the video was "inconclusive". Even so, it was intriguing. The video presented a fisheye view of the mummy exhibit's largest room, with the mystery mummy's glass chamber in the centre. The chamber looked much further away than it actually was, like a reflection in a rear-view mirror. At the same time, the camera's night-vision technology lent the black-and-white video an eerie quality, almost as though they were seeing the images in negative.

The video, which was coded in twenty-four-hour military time, spanned roughly three hours – from the moment the museum closed to the moment the kids discovered that the mummy was missing – but it was sped up to play in under ten minutes. The first three-quarters or so showed almost no movement at all. Then,

guitarsamurai: hey, what was that? wait – *is rewinding*

guitarsamurai: there, at 19:36:15...those stars – I didn't see them before...

survivor 3000: oh, you mean like those lights on the glass?

juniorjester: that's just reflection.

guitarsamurai: yeah, but of what? the mummy's ghost!? lol

survivor3000: ha-ha.

guitarsamurai: seriously, it's not yr flashlight – we don't come for another three min. and guard wasn't there yet. can't be like car lights or anything from outside – no window.

survivor3000: maybe the thief's flashlight?

guitarsamurai: maybe.

juniorjester: a flashlight would just be a single light, not like a bunch of little ones – unless maybe it bounced off some stuff? but there wasn't anything reflective besides glass.

survivor3000: he could have been wearing a headlamp and holding a flashlight. or there could have been somebody else with one, too.

juniorjester: there are more lights than that.

guitarsamurai: all right, forget the lights. let's move on to the guy.

They each forwarded to the man who exited the glass chamber about three minutes before they arrived. Several times already, they had watched this shadowy figure walk out of the exhibit – and out of the picture frame – but they hadn't yet come up with a plausible explanation for his actions. Presumably, this was the man (or, possibly, woman – you couldn't see the face in the darkness) who had stolen the mummy. And yet there appeared to be no way he could have the mummy with him. His hands were empty. He carried no bag. He wore no backpack. And it seemed hardly credible that the mummy was hidden in his clothes. The man looked too skinny, too gaunt. Surely, there would have been at least one tell-tale lump if he had slipped the mummy under his shirt.

What's more, he was never seen entering the mummy's chamber, only leaving it.

guitarsamurai: hey, I have an idea – what if mummy was stolen earlier in the day, and this guy lied down in the mummy's place – then got up later after exhibit closed?
survivor3000: yeah, that fits. Kind of like putting pillows in your bed so your parents will think you're sleeping. m-e?
juniorjester: *thinking*

survivor3000: take your time, we've got all night…not.

juniorjester: okay, done. sorry, not realistic. that would mean (a) even with all those people coming to see the show, nobody noticed mummy being stolen, and then (b) afterwards nobody noticed that there was a living guy instead of a mummy in the sarcophagus.

guitarsamurai: why u have to be such a doubter, man? maybe he had really good Halloween make-up?

survivor3000: m-e is right. remember what the mummy looked like? that would be hard to fake.

survivor3000: but it's a theory, anyway – maybe enough to get us out of trouble?

Max-Ernest was torn. In some ways, Yo-Yoji's theory was a good one; it reminded him of one of those locked-room mysteries that seem impossible to solve but then turn out to have a nifty resolution that's been staring you in the face the whole time. Still, he didn't like the theory – and not *just* because it was Yo-Yoji's and not his. Something was nagging at him. He decided to apply the deductive reasoning of the master of the locked-room mystery, Sherlock Holmes.

juniorjester: maybe we're looking at this the wrong way.

guitarsamurai: okay...?

juniorjester: well, Sherlock Holmes always said, when you have eliminated the impossible, whatever remains, however improbable, must be the truth.

survivor3000: yeah, so?

juniorjester: what do we actually know? that somebody walked out of the mummy chamber. and that later the mummy was missing, right?

juniorjester: and nobody walked IN except us.

survivor3000: get to the point.

juniorjester: you know how it seems like the problem is that the thief walks out but he doesn't have the mummy with him? what if it's actually the reverse?

survivor3000: what do you mean?

juniorjester: what if there wasn't a break-IN at all? what if there was...a break-OUT?

guitarsamurai: just say it, dude.

juniorjester: okay, okay, what if what we're looking at is not a thief walking out without a mummy but the mummy walking out without a thief?

Max-Ernest stared at his computer screen, unable to believe what he'd just written. He, Max-Ernest, with the logical mind. But that was the conclusion that logic had drawn him to.

Cass and Yo-Yoji seemed unable to believe it as well.

survivor3000: u saying what I think ur saying?

guitarsamurai: okay, when are u going to say april fools?

juniorjester: that was a few weeks ago.

survivor3000: u serious?

juniorjester: I'm serious. I think. No, wait, that would mean I was completely crazy... I don't know.

guitarsamurai: just a sec, I'm going to get a screen capture, then enlarge it.

Yo-Yoji enlarged the image of the man almost to the point where he was more pixel than person. His face was still too dark to see, but something near the bottom of the image caught Yo-Yoji's eye and made him hold his breath. Without alerting his friends, he e-mailed each of them a copy of the enlarged image with this subject line: LOOK BEHIND HIS RIGHT FOOT.

That was where the strip of linen could be seen trailing from the man's trouser leg.

The man leaving the exhibit was the mummy. The mummy was walking.

A Head Wrapped
in Bandages

Elsewhere that evening, in a luxurious hotel suite, a beautiful woman in a shimmering white gown looked out a tall window at the city lights below. Her face, reflected in the glass, was as pale as snow, her eyes as cold as ice. Her blonde hair, shiny and unmoving, curled outwards at the ends like the petals of a flower frozen in mid-bloom. And yet at the waist, her body curved inwards to an almost impossible degree, as if all the air had been squeezed out of her, along with all the warmth. Only her hands, hidden by long white gloves, moved even a tiny bit. They were splayed on the window, trembling slightly, as if she wanted nothing more than to grasp the city below and make it her own.

Yes, it was Ms. Mauvais.*

"Tell me why you are here," she said, her voice as soft and comforting as shattered glass. "Surely you have not risen from the dead just to say hello?"

The only response was laboured breathing – like the sound of a lung patient on a respirator – and a faint gasp of helplessness.

Then, as if from far away, came a voice. It was dry and raspy and muffled. Each word was a cry of despair. "I...need...your...help."

---

*I KNOW, YOU RECOGNIZED HER IMMEDIATELY. THE LONG DESCRIPTION WASN'T NECESSARY; I JUST FELT LIKE WRITING IT.

Ms. Mauvais regarded the reflection behind her own. Over her shoulder, a head was just visible, wrapped in long white bandages. Haunted eyes stared out between the strips of linen.

"Yes, my darling creature?"

"It's…my…skin."

"That's why you came all the way to see me? A few blemishes?"

"Not just a few!" the creature protested. "It's really bad. I can't live with myself."

Ms. Mauvais turned to face her visitor.

Below the mummy-like head were the clothes of a fashionable young girl: a twin♥hearts™ T-shirt, skinny jeans and ballet flats.

"Now, now – of course you can't, darling. Your skin is your skin. It's irreplaceable…almost." Ms. Mauvais laughed mirthlessly. "Nothing is of more intimate concern than one's outward appearance. I myself once crossed two continents to have a single wrinkle removed." She pointed to her plaster-smooth forehead. "You can't see it now, can you?"

The girl standing in front of Ms. Mauvais shook her head – as best she could, given the bandages criss-crossing her face.

Ms. Mauvais regarded her sceptically. "Amanda, isn't it?"

"Amber," said the girl. The bandages puffed in and out with each syllable.

"Of course, how silly of me. Amanda. It's so nice … not to see you again."

"Please help me. Please. My doctor gave me something, but it almost made me blind." Amber started to sob.

"You realize crying is only going to make it worse – it reddens the cheeks," said Ms. Mauvais without a trace of sympathy. "Well, let's have a look –"

Amber slowly unpeeled the bandages and revealed her face, leaving the strips in a sticky heap on the carpet.

It was a face that would have struck terror into the hearts of boys and girls of a certain age everywhere.

The acne started at Amber's hairline and didn't stop until it reached her collarbone; it covered so much of her face that only her eyeballs were unblemished. It was as if her acne had acne. There were whiteheads and blackheads and big, bloody redheads. There were pimples on top of pimples on top of pimples. Some were deeply buried like dormant volcanoes. Others had just risen to the surface, fiery mountains aching to burst. Still others had already erupted, leaving trails of zit-lava smeared across Amber's epidermal layer – gooey evidence of the tumultuous geothermal activity underneath. The few bits of clear skin that remained were red and raw from all the scratching and scraping and squeezing and tweezing. It was painful to look at her.

Expressionless, Ms. Mauvais studied Amber for a moment.

"Thank you. That's enough." She motioned for Amber to put the bandages back on. "It's worse than I imagined. I hope those bandages hold up. You may want to put a paper bag over your head just in case."

"Can you...fix me?" asked Amber. She did her best to re-wrap herself, using the window as a mirror.

"Can I...or will I?"

There was a knock on the door. An exceptionally tall and broad woman – she could have been a basketball player or a rugby player, her choice – shuffled in.

"Yes, Daisy?"

"I have...a message," said Daisy hesitantly. "Should I wait?" She nodded meaningfully in Amber's direction.

"No need to worry about her." Ms. Mauvais waved her hand dismissively, as if Amber were of no more consequence than a potted plant.

"It's about those kids—"

"Which kids? There are so many these days."

"You know which," said Daisy, her brow furrowed in irritation. "Cassandra and her gang."

"Oh, them," said Ms. Mauvais without betraying the slightest bit of emotion. "Are they still kids? One feels they should be old by now – they've already caused so much vexation in their short, meaningless little lives."

"Lord Pharaoh says they have something he wants. He says you'll know what it is."

"I see."

"Don't you want me to...get it for you?" Daisy's gloved hands clutched at each other as if she were already anticipating wringing the necks of her young victims.

"No, I do not!" snapped Ms. Mauvais. "I told you to stay out of the way, all of you."

"As you wish, Madame," said Daisy, disappointed.

"Now get out, you pathetic oaf."

As Daisy shuffled out, Ms. Mauvais turned back to Amber. "Amanda, dear, perhaps I will help you after all."

Amber whimpered hopefully.

The Mummy's Laugh

"**W**HO PULLED OFF MY FINGER? I WANT MY FINGER!"

The woods were cold and grey, the trees bare and ashen.

Yo-Yoji ran faster and faster. But the voice behind him kept getting louder and louder.

"WHO PULLED OFF MY FINGER? I WANT MY FINGER!"

"I didn't mean to take it!" Yo-Yoji shouted over his shoulder. "Cass just threw it to me!"

He could hear twigs breaking, leaves crunching. His own footsteps or his pursuer's? He couldn't tell.

"FIN-GER! I. WANT. MY. FINGER!"

"The museum has it! I'll get it back for you, I promise."

"FIN-GER...FINGER FINGER FINGER!"

"Just let me live! Please!"

He tripped on a rock and fell to the ground. Winded and terrified, he looked up into the dark yawning mouth of –

"PULL MY FINGER! I WANT YOU TO PULL MY FINGER!"

– his little brother, Gajin, in his Spider-Man Underoos. Not as scary a sight as the mouth of a mummy, perhaps, but equally unwelcome.

"Pull my finger!" repeated Gajin, pointing his finger at his sleepy older brother.

"Go away," said Yo-Yoji, closing his eyes.

"Pull my finger!"

"Go away."

"Not until you pull my finger."

"What? Why?"

"Just pull my finger, *please*."

"Fine, but then you're leaving my room."

Yo-Yoji lifted his head off his pillow and gave his brother's index finger a quick tug.

Gajin grinned and let out a loud fart.

"Thanks, I needed that!" he said with exaggerated relief, and then started laughing hysterically.

"Dude, you're worse than Max-Ernest," Yo-Yoji groaned.

Gajin shrugged. "Mom says you're going to be late for school!" he shouted, running out of his older brother's room.

Max-Ernest was the last to arrive. The other students were bent over their desks, taking a test.

"Sorry I'm late," he said to his maths teacher, who was writing something on the chalkboard. "I—"

Max-Ernest had a momentary memory lapse. Why *was* he late? But his teacher appeared not to notice. At least, he didn't turn around.

Slightly unnerved, Max-Ernest sat down. His test was on his desk, along with a pencil. How could he have forgotten there was a test today? It was so unlike him.

When he saw what was written on the test, he frowned. There weren't any words or numbers, only symbols. Hieroglyphs. Strange that they would be on a maths test, although, of course, the ancient Egyptians were very good at maths.

He glanced around the classroom. He could read hieroglyphs, yes, but surely the other students would not be expected to translate from ancient Egyptian. Could this be a message written only for him?

Max-Ernest scrutinized the hieroglyphs, trying to make sense of them.

"S-EE-K-R-E-T," he sounded out. *Secret.*

For a second, he was thrilled with his discovery. Then he realized that this couldn't be the Secret they were looking for; it was just the modern word, rendered phonetically in hieroglyphs. Was somebody playing a joke on him? Taunting him?

He looked up. The teacher was walking towards

him. Wearing the clothes of a maths teacher, he had the face of –

– the mummy!

The mummy grinned at Max-Ernest, revealing the dark hole inside his head. "Congratulations, Max-Ernest – you figured it out!"

The mummy extended his four-fingered hand. Terrified, Max-Ernest shook the mummy's hand, only to experience the electrifying jolt of –

– his alarm clock. It was time to get up.

"Cassandra, my dear, come, get off your ear—"

The Jester looked down at Cass with concerned eyes. The bells on his hat gently jingled. Around them, the red-and-white-striped sides of his tent billowed in the wind.

"Time is running out. Stop lying about."

Cass raised her head. "How long do I have?" she asked, fighting the sense of panic that was overtaking her.

In answer, the Jester picked up an hourglass off a card table and turned it over.

As the sand began to pour, the sides of the tent gave way and flew up in the wind as if they were as light as paper. . .

Cass blinked. When she opened her eyes, the Jester was gone and she was standing in a vast and silent desert.

Ahead of her, a black-and-white bird – an ibis – flew in slow circles above an enormous sand dune. Cass could feel the bird's dark eyes on her. Waiting for her.

She started walking towards the dune, her bare feet sliding backwards in the sand with every step. On her finger, the gold ibis ring pulsed. It felt warm.

Soon, Cass thought, soon I will know the Secret. The points of her ears prickled in anticipation.

Suddenly, a hot wind stirred the sand and forced the bird to flap his wings harder. The bird's movements became erratic, his circles larger.

The wind got stronger and stronger until sand was blowing in big gusts off the top of the dune. The sand stung Cass's eyes. It blew into her mouth, her ears, her hair.

The ibis could no longer hold his position. With a single, plaintive cry in Cass's direction, he flew off into the horizon.

Protecting her face as well as she could, Cass trudged forwards, determined to reach the dune. But the closer she got, the smaller the dune became; it was as if she were falling further away rather than coming closer.

By the time she reached the spot where the dune had been, there was only flat desert.

And, lying exposed on the ground, the mummy.

He sat up and looked at her; his eyes were the eyes of the ibis.

"What is the Secret?" she shouted, but her voice was lost in the wind.

She tried to repeat her question, but this time the words would not leave her lips.

She stumbled, then tried to regain her footing, then stumbled again. The wind knocked her flat. She could feel sand blowing onto her, burying her. Soon only her face and right hand were uncovered. Sand swirled around the ibis ring as if simultaneously attracted and repelled by opposing magnetic forces.

The mummy stood over her. Behind him, loose linen bandages blew in the wind.

"The Secret? You want me to tell *you* the Secret?" He started to laugh. "*You* have the ring. Give me the ring!"

He laughed harder and harder until she was entirely covered in sand and about to choke.

She woke up with her face buried in her pillow and the mummy's ring pulling at the chain around her neck.

The
Curious Case
of the
Walking Mummy

GRADUATION SPEECH – SECOND DRAFT
by M-E

TITLE:

~~THE MUMMY MYSTERY~~
~~M IS FOR MUMMY~~
~~MUMMY DEAREST~~
~~ARE YOU MY MUMMY?~~
~~THE MUMMY'S SECRET~~
~~SECRETS OF THE MYSTERY MUMMY~~
~~THE CURSE OF THE MUMMY'S FINGER~~
~~THE MISSING MUMMY MYSTERY~~
~~THE MYSTERY OF THE MISSING MUMMY~~
~~THE MYSTERY MUMMY GOES MISSING~~
~~THE MYSTERY MUMMY RISES AGAIN~~
~~NIGHT OF THE LIVING MUMMY~~
~~THE GREAT MUMMY ESCAPE~~

THE CURIOUS CASE OF THE WALKING
MUMMY

(Yes! sounds most Sherlock Holmes-ish)

OPENING JOKE:
Find later. Not in mood. (You? Not in mood for

joke?? What happened – feeling mum? Missing your mummy? Ha-ha!)

THESIS:

When you have eliminated the impossible, whatever remains must be the truth.

SPEECH:

Unlike Cass, who likes novels, especially adventure stories like *Robinson Crusoe* and *The Count of Monte Cristo*, I usually like non-fiction. (Wait, why am I talking about Cass in my graduation speech? Bad beginning. Erase. Emergency. *Errr...* *Sound of brakes squealing*) Starting over...

In my opinion, non-fiction makes more sense and is more informative than fiction.*

The only genre of fiction I like is the mystery. (*Genre* means *kind of fiction*, if you don't know.) Mystery novels, such as the ones by Sherlock Holmes, are like long puzzles that you can work out in your head. (You mean ones *about* Sherlock Holmes, duh. Sir Arthur Conan Doyle is the writer!)

---

*I THINK MOST PEOPLE WOULD AGREE. THE QUESTION IS WHETHER THOSE ARE DESIRABLE TRAITS IN A BOOK.

But every once in a while, you find a mystery that you can't work out because there's some kind of supernatural element involved. I'm not necessarily a big fan of those mysteries, but I guess a lot of people are.

In most mummy stories, for example, a mummy rises from the dead for one of the following reasons:

– curse or magical spell
– revenge
– reunion with a wife or lover
– a combination of the above

But none of these are very realistic, are they?

If a mummy truly has been reanimated – so that he's actually walking!! – there must be a more rational explanation. Right? I mean, right?? An explanation that fits the laws of nature, not the laws of literature.

What does this have to do with graduation? Nothing. But it's important to think about because... well, you never know...

The Library

Max-Ernest was so preoccupied with the Curious Case of the Walking Mummy (the actual case, not his graduation speech) that he'd almost forgotten he had detention on Monday morning.

Luckily, when he tried to sit down at the Nuts Table at recess, Glob and Daniel-not-Danielle were there to remind Max-Ernest of his pitiable fate. They felt so sorry for him that they fortified him with a new pizza-flavoured energy bar and an old *Silver Surfer* comic, respectively, before steering him towards his place of confinement – the school library.

The library had once been Max-Ernest's favourite place on campus. When he was in the lower grades and hadn't yet become friends with Cass and Yo-Yoji, the books in the library provided a refuge from the confusing world of the playground. In those days, other kids always seemed to him to be speaking in code – a code he couldn't crack, no matter how many methods he applied. Books, on the other hand, he could rely on to explain themselves; and if a book used a word he didn't know, he could always look up the definition.

He used to sit in the corner of the library reading and rereading first the Hardy Boys and Nancy Drew, later Sir Arthur Conan Doyle and Edgar Allan Poe. As he read, he would imagine he was an apprentice investigator hired to assist the detective heroes, never guessing that he would soon be solving mysteries of his own as a member of a top secret international organization – the Terces Society.

Today, as he entered the library, he could see hardly a trace of the room he remembered. The old librarian, Pam, had retired a year before, and budget cuts meant that she had yet to be replaced. Gone were Pam's more eccentric shelf labels, like BOOKS TO READ WHEN YOU'RE SICK and BOOKS FOR BOYS WHO LIKE BUGS and BOOKS THAT SMELL LIKE OLD SHOES and A BOOK A DAY KEEPS THE DOCTOR AWAY. The only posters that remained on the walls were strict admonishments about the virtues (rather than the pleasures) of reading.

In any event, there was no question of Max-Ernest's picking up a new mystery to read right now. Whether he liked it or not, he was more than sufficiently occupied with a mystery already – a mummy mystery. And a doozy of a mummy mystery at that.

Mrs. Johnson came out from behind the librarian's desk when he walked in.

"Sit!" She pointed to a table where Cass was already seated and writing in her notebook. "Dr. Ndefo hasn't yet told me what happened at the museum, but I understand things did not go well. I'm sure I will learn all the details soon. In the meantime, I want you to work on your graduation speech and reflect on the terrible fate that awaits you should I choose not to let you graduate. Not only will you have to relive the current year – with me – but you will, in all likelihood, be dooming yourself to a lifetime of crime and poverty. Homelessness, hunger, early death – these are things you can look forward to..."

Max-Ernest nodded, gulping. "You forgot prison."

"Where do you think you are now? And rest assured, I will be back to check on you, so no funny business," she added as she walked out.

Max-Ernest hadn't seen Cass since watching the video, and there were many things he wanted to say when he walked up to her, but instead of blurting everything out at once, he extended his hand.

"Shake."

"Why?" asked Cass, shutting her notebook. She couldn't remember the last time they'd shaken hands – if they ever had.

"Just do it."

Warily, Cass took his hand – then jerked hers away. "What was that? Did you take my ring?!"

"No. Look –"

He opened his palm and revealed a round metal disc with a button in the middle. Cass looked at it as though it might be the trigger for a bomb. "And that is . . . ?"

"A hand buzzer. It's a prank. Very old school. You know, like a whoopee cushion or a squirt ring. Anyway, it's got a spring inside. I thought maybe that's how the ibis ring works. How 'bout that?"

"So you think the ring is a prank, too?" asked Cass dubiously. "A joke ring? From ancient Egypt?"

Max-Ernest shrugged. "Well, Dr. Amun liked cartoons, right? Maybe he liked pranks, too." He wasn't about to tell her he got the idea from his dream. "Where is Yo-Yoji, by the way?"

"No idea. Maybe he got so spooked by the idea of a walking mummy that he's dropping out of school and we're never going to see him again."

"Yo-Yoji? I doubt it."

They were silent for a moment. For reasons that had only partially to do with a walking mummy and an ancient secret, talking wasn't as easy between them as it had been even a short time before.

Max-Ernest eyed her notebook. "Is the you-know-what in there? I mean, the hieroglyphs?"

Cass hesitated.

"Blink once for yes, twice for no."

Cass rolled her eyes.

"That's okay, you don't have to tell me. You don't have to show it to me. You don't have to do anything you don't want to do." He had practised these words in his head, and he felt he had delivered them with admirable calm.

Cass looked at him. "You get that it's not because I don't want to, right?"

"You don't? I mean, it's not?" Max-Ernest couldn't look her in the eye.

"No, you dummy. Haven't you noticed I keep asking for your help even though I can't really talk about...it. I can't do this without you; you know that. You were the one who found the ring in the trunk, remember?"

"I didn't think you'd noticed," said Max-Ernest, trying not to choke up. "Actually, if you want to know the truth, I didn't think you really wanted to be friends any more."

"What? That's—"

"Ridiculous?"

They both laughed.

"Okay, now that's settled. So what do you think... it...is?" asked Cass.

Max-Ernest shook his head. "I have no idea. But the walking mummy? I can't help feeling he must have something to do with...it."

Cass looked at her friend in surprise. He didn't usually put much stock in feelings, only facts. "So then you think the mummy really came back to life?" she asked. "You, Mr. Rational?"

"I didn't say that exactly."

"Hey, wait, I just thought of something," said Cass excitedly. Quickly, she opened her notebook and peeked inside, careful not to let Max-Ernest see what she was looking at. "Is there a hieroglyph that looks like feet? And could it mean *walk*?"

"Yes, there's a hieroglyph that looks like feet – there's one that looks like pretty much everything. And sometimes it means *walk*. I think it can also mean *run*, *cross*, *move*, *go* – whatever makes sense for where it is."

Cass wrote notes as Max-Ernest talked. "Forget I'm telling you this," she said, "but for a long time, I thought the last hieroglyph of the…it…just looked like a letter *V*. But now that I think about it, I sort of drew the *V* with feet. Maybe the feet were the important part of the hieroglyph, and I just didn't realize it."

"So you're thinking that the you-know-what is about walking – and therefore that's what made the mummy walk? I thought it was about an ibis or Thoth." Max-Ernest couldn't hide his scepticism.

145

"So then what's your theory about what it is?" asked Cass, closing her notebook. "I know you have one. You always do."

Max-Ernest shrugged.

In truth, he did not have a theory about what the Secret was. Not currently. For a long time, he had suspected that the Secret might have something to do with the legendary philosopher's stone – the magical substance that was the holy grail of alchemy and that turned lead into gold and made people immortal. More recently, however, he'd begun to doubt this theory. The philosopher's stone was a European myth. The Secret, on the other hand, had originated in ancient Egypt. Didn't it therefore make sense to look for the Secret in Egyptian mythology?

He thought he might have hit on something when he read about the *Book of Thoth* – a book said to contain all the spells of the universe. But what, then, would the Secret be? If the Secret came from the *Book of Thoth*, it literally could be about anything.

"No, I know it's hard to believe, but I really don't have a theory," he said.

"Yoo-hoo!"

For a second, neither of them recognized the giddy

girl bouncing through the door with a sheepish Yo-Yoji in tow.

"Hi, guys! Did y'all miss me?"

"Amber?!" Cass and Max-Ernest cried out at the same time.

Amber appeared transformed, and yet the most astonishing thing about her transformation was how much like herself she still looked; she was just a better, more beautiful version of the Amber they'd known for years. All traces of acne gone, her skin was smoother than ever, with a new hint of pink on her cheeks and a new dewiness on her lips. Her eyes sparkled; her smile effervesced. Her hair shimmered, and when she tossed it, it seemed to float in slow motion like a shampoo commercial brought to life. There was something dazzling and unreal about her; she was a mirage of youthful perfection.

"What happened to you?" asked Max-Ernest. "We heard you went blind or something."

"Is that what people are saying?" Amber laughed – a tinkly laugh that chilled her schoolmates without their quite knowing why. "I just had a little cold, that's all. So sorry to keep your friend out of detention. Mrs. Johnson said I could borrow him for a moment." Amber smiled at Yo-Yoji. "I know it was torture for him...right, Yo-Yoji?"

Yo-Yoji didn't say anything, but his cheeks flushed red.

"*Borrow* him? He's not a library book," said Cass, stone-faced.

"It's just that he's so good with graphics and computers and stuff, and I needed to make posters for Grad Night," said Amber breezily. "See?" She held up a flyer with a picture of King Tut's mask on it. "Doesn't it look awesome? *Ridiculous*, right?"

Max-Ernest noted silently that Amber had used Yo-Yoji's word without apparent effort.

"Oh, yeah, totally *ridiculous*," imitated Cass, obviously noting the same thing – not so silently.

"The theme is going to be King Tut," Amber blithely continued. "You know, 'Dance like an Egyptian'? We've been practising." She demonstrated, bending her arms and wrists at right angles, and thrusting one hand forwards and one hand back. "C'mon, Yo-Yoji. Show them."

Blushing even harder, Yo-Yoji put his hands in position and started doing the Egyptian dance.

Amber smiled at Cass and Max-Ernest. "Cool, huh?"

Max-Ernest winced. It wasn't that dancing like an Egyptian was necessarily *un*cool – Max-Ernest didn't feel qualified to make that judgment one way or the other. It was just seeing Yo-Yoji reduced to following Amber's orders. It was more disturbing than when Yo-Yoji had been in the grip of a seventeenth-century samurai.

"Why don't you guys try?" Amber suggested.

Cass and Max-Ernest shook their heads: not a chance.

With Amber's attention directed at the others, Yo-Yoji pointed at Amber as if to say, *Don't look at me, look at her*. But somehow that only made it worse.

Max-Ernest looked at Cass to see how she was responding to the humiliation of their friend. Her face remained calm, but her ears were a fiery crimson.

Indeed, a lot of thoughts were racing through Cass's head at the moment – most of them unrepeatable in polite company. But one question was paramount: what had happened to Amber?

"Speaking of the dance, do you guys have any Egyptian stuff?" asked Amber casually. "Like, maybe some costumes or something left over from the Egypt unit?"

"My costume was paper, and it ripped when both my parents tried to take it," said Max-Ernest truthfully.

"What about you, Cass, don't you have anything?" asked Amber.

Cass shook her head, staring at Amber.

The only other person Cass knew to have changed so dramatically was their friend Benjamin Blake, and his transformation had been courtesy of the Midnight Sun. Come to think of it, the new Amber reminded Cass very much of a young Ms. Mauvais...

"Maybe some jewellery," Amber persisted. "Like a bracelet or a ring or something?"

"What would you want a ring for?" asked Cass, a vague suspicion beginning to form in her mind.

"Oh, I was just thinking, you know, like for a prize, or for the queen of the dance or something. Not for me, if that's what you were thinking," said Amber with a laugh. "Why? Do you have an Egyptian ring you could loan us? It would be awesome if you did."

While Amber spoke, Yo-Yoji kept motioning behind her back. At first Cass thought he was still doing the Egyptian dance, but then she realized Yo-Yoji was trying to point to something. After looking Amber up and down and then up again, Cass figured out what it was: the silver tote bag hanging from Amber's shoulder.

"Hey, Amber, where did you get that bag?" she asked.

At the top of the bag was a tag bearing an insignia of a black sun and the words SOLAR-ZERO LLC.

"Um, I got it in – actually, I don't remember," Amber stammered, her bubbly ease momentarily fizzing. "I think it was my mom's. I could try to get you one if you like it," she added, recovering.

"That's okay. I just thought I recognized the name." Cass looked significantly at her friends as Amber walked quickly away.

Max-Ernest's eyes widened. "That's it! I knew it was a weird name. Zero in twenty-four-hour time is midnight."

Cass nodded. "And *solar* means..."

The three friends looked at each other, acknowledging the awful fact: SOLAR-ZERO LLC was the Midnight Sun.

Which meant the Midnight Sun had financed the mummy exhibit.

Which meant the mummy's arrival in their lives – and his mysterious departure – was no coincidence at all.

It was something much worse.

CHAPTER SIXTEEN

A Visitor at the Circus

It was just before noon. The sun was high, but the circus was still quiet.

A handsome, impeccably dressed man with a cool, unruffled demeanour strolled along the midway, his hands casually resting in his coat pockets.

At first glance, he couldn't have looked more out of place in these decidedly scruffy surroundings. The trash-strewn ground had likely never been trod upon by shoes as shiny as his. The tattered tents were almost an insult to his smooth tanned skin. And behind the rusty bars of an ancient cage, the mangy mane of a once-regal lion seemed to wilt in the light of the man's perfectly coiffed silver hair.

But if you happened to look closely at his eyes, you might have read there a different story. They were the eyes of a much older man – much older than this man at first appeared. You could see the telltale beginnings of crow's feet around the corners, and the whites of his eyes had a slightly yellowish cast. But it wasn't simply a question of age; it was also the emotion in his eyes – the tears. The sight of the circus moved him, it seemed, reminding him of his lost youth, perhaps, or of something or someone from his past.

Possibly, it was this memory that caused him to stop in front of a greasy old popcorn cart and close his eyes for a moment.

He mumbled to himself. Four words. They sounded like a spell or an incantation. Or a very odd recipe.

"Heliotrope... Echinacea... Liquorice... Peanut butter..."

When he opened his eyes, two clowns – or at least two men who had been made up as clowns the night before (and hadn't washed their faces since) – stood in front of him.

"Admission is ten dollars," said the skinnier, taller clown whose name was Morrie. "Exact change only."

"Well, if you want to give us a hundred dollars, that's okay, too," said the shorter, fatter clown, Mickey. "Just don't expect any change back."

"Oh, I don't know, for a hundred, we can give him *something* back. How about a smile?"

Mickey grinned. "Right. No change. Except the change in our moods. Nothing sadder than a sad clown."

"Why should I pay anything?" asked the visitor. "The circus is closed."

Morrie nodded. "I couldn't have said it better myself! The circus is closed. You pay, we open it for you."

"And do what? A clown act? I'm getting that for free."

"Oh, so now you think you can make fun of us, huh, wise guy?" Mickey growled.

"Yeah, mister, we make the jokes around here!" growled Morrie. "Your job is to be the butt of them."

The visitor chuckled. "Easy, friends. For your information, I'm not some rube walking into the circus so you can make me into your next mark."

"Well, you're not some old carny, either – I can tell you that much," said Mickey, studying the well-groomed man in front of him. "Not with that fancy, sort-of-European-sort-of-not accent of yours."

"Yeah, where you from anyway – Paris, Texas?" asked Morrie.

Mickey laughed. "Good one, Morrie."

Morrie took a bow. "Thanks, Mickey. I perform here every night. Tell your friends."

"I'm here to see Pietro," said the visitor, losing patience. "Can you tell me where he is?"

At the mention of the circus master's name, the clowns relaxed slightly.

"Pietro? Why didn't you say so?" exclaimed Mickey.

"And who should we say is calling at this god-awful hour?" asked Morrie.

"It's noon."

"That's *high* noon to you," Morrie corrected.

"And bedtime for us," Mickey added.

"Tell him a...relative is here to see him."

"Relative, huh? Come to think of it, you do look kind of like the old man," said Morrie. "Sort of the newer, shinier version."

Mickey nodded. "Kind of like when they take those classic old cars and reissue them fifty years later."

"What are you, his nephew or something?" asked Morrie.

"Actually, I'm his twin brother," said the visitor, extending his hand for the first time. "Doctor Luciano Bergamo, at your service."

"His brother?!" exclaimed the clowns in unison.

Neither clown moved to shake the man's hand. They just stared in disbelief at his pristine white glove.

CHAPTER SEVENTEEN

Hobo Marks

The revelation that the Midnight Sun had financed the mummy exhibit certainly added an interesting wrinkle to the Curious Case of the Walking Mummy. It meant that the Midnight Sun knew who Dr. Amun was and that they wanted the mummy nearby. That much was clear. What confounded Max-Ernest as he walked home that afternoon was the question of whether or not they were now in possession of the mummy.

He saw three possibilities:

One, the Midnight Sun had broken into the museum and taken the mummy. If so, why were they not on the video?

Two (and he was hesitant to believe this), the Midnight Sun had somehow managed to resurrect the mummy. The mummy had then left the museum according to their instructions and was now their zombie slave.

Three (equally unlikely), their plan had backfired. The mummy had come back to life – whether with the Midnight Sun's help or on his own – and had then walked out of his own accord. In this case, the mummy was now roaming the world as a rogue agent.

Max-Ernest didn't accept any of these possibilities, but no matter how much he thought about it, he couldn't think of any others.

Thinking, as you probably know from experience, can be very hazardous to your health. I don't mean that thinking may lead you to do something hazardous (like investigate secrets), although of course that's true as well. I mean thinking can cause you physical harm.

On the best of days, Max-Ernest was prone to walking into things: walls, cars, telephone poles, fire hydrants, people carrying trays of food or bags of groceries. When he was deep in thought, as he was now, he was liable to walk off a cliff.

Luckily, the drop from the kerb to the street was only a few centimetres. Still, it was sufficient to cause him to trip and fall and lie sprawled on the asphalt cogitating anxiously about all the possible sprains and abrasions and breaks and bruises that he might or might not just now or in the future be suffering from.

The view from ground level is seldom pleasant – unless you happen to be lying in a meadow or on a sandy beach – but it can be revelatory. Sometimes when we are at our lowest points, we make our greatest discoveries. Not so Max-Ernest. Eyes blurred, cheeks scraped, Max-Ernest stared across the street to the empty parking lot on the other side. He waited for some profound realization. It didn't come. (Thankfully, neither did any cars.) He did, however, see something that caused his pulse to quicken:

A movement in the bushes.

And – what was that? An arm? A leg?

Then…nothing.

Max-Ernest's first instinct was to stay where he was and play dead. Then he realized that was silly. If there was someone – a reanimated mummy, for example, or more likely his reanimated schoolmate, Amber – who wanted to attack him, he would be far more vulnerable lying in the street than standing up. And even if nobody meant him any harm, there was still the probability of being run over.

Reluctantly, he stood.

Imagining that Cass was watching – and judging – his actions, he resisted running home and instead walked across the street to investigate.

"Hello?" The word came out as a screech.

Nobody answered. There was no sound of any kind.

Until a pigeon flew out from behind a bush.

Max-Ernest looked around, feeling rather foolish.

His mother's house – or, more accurately, his mother's half house – had stood here in this lot during the time it was separated from his father's half house. Max-Ernest remembered that time well: a hopeful time when it seemed for once that his parents might live like normal divorced parents – that is, separately. Now that his mother's half house had rejoined his father's (and his parents were once again cohabiting and once again not speaking to each other), all that remained in the place of his mother's half house were a half dozen or so slabs of cement and a variety of sad-looking weeds.

Usually, nothing decorated the surface of the cement except dead leaves and the occasional splatter of bird droppings. Today, however, he saw something more intriguing.

He looked around to make sure he was unobserved. Then he leaned down to inspect the cement more closely. Yes, there they were, faint but unmistakable: two symbols drawn in chalk.

Hieroglyphs! Could it be a message left for him by the mummy? This time real and not dreamed.

He looked again. No, it wasn't a message from the mummy.

Still, the markings looked very similar to hieroglyphs, and in a general sense they *were* hieroglyphs. Not ancient Egyptian hieroglyphs but modern ones.

They were hobo marks – a written code used by hobos to communicate secretly with one another, often offering warnings and advice.*

To most people, the marks at Max-Ernest's feet would mean nothing. Even to a hobo, they would appear contradictory, if not downright crazy.

Literally translated, the two symbols meant:

GO QUICKLY / FLEE –
STAY / SAFE PLACE TO SPEND NIGHT

To members of the Terces Society, however, they meant something quite different:

URGENT –
MEET TONIGHT AT HEADQUARTERS

Max-Ernest walked home with a furrowed brow.

Why was Pietro calling in the troops? They'd been sending him regular reports on the mummy situation, but maybe he wanted to hear about it in person. Or perhaps Pietro had some information for them.

In either case, Max-Ernest welcomed the chance

---

*A HOBO IS A WANDERING VAGABOND WHO TRAVELS BY TRAIN. NOT TO BE CONFUSED WITH A TRAMP, WHO USUALLY TRAVELS BY FOOT, "TRAMPING" ALONG ROADS.

to talk to the old magician. No doubt he would provide new insight into the Curious Case of the Walking Mummy.

Shortly before midnight, Max-Ernest stood across the street from Cass's house, anxiously checking his watch. Pietro was the kind of man whose favourite form of relaxation consisted of fixing old clocks so they kept perfect time; he didn't like it when people were late.

Max-Ernest felt a tap on his shoulder. Flinching, he turned around – all the way around – until he saw Cass smiling mischievously at him.

"Just a little taste of your own medicine. Hope I didn't scare you...too much."

"Only because you're late," he replied irritably. "Three minutes and forty-two seconds later than last time. You should practise climbing out your bedroom window more often."

"And you should stop looking at your watch. I've been standing right behind you for longer than that."

"Really?"

"No, but I might have been. You should be more careful."

He opened his mouth, trying to think of a snappy comeback, when Yo-Yoji walked up.

"Hey."

"Hey," said his friends.

"Sorry about in the library today," said Yo-Yoji. "I know that was kinda goofy. Mrs. Johnson made me go with Amber and then—"

"What are you sorry for? People like who they like," said Cass.

"I don't *like* her. When I saw her bag, I decided to be nice to find out if she knew anything."

"Whatever you say."

"Why you have to be like that, dude?"

"Like what? Dude."

"Um, guys," said Max-Ernest, trying and failing to get their attention.

"I just think you should be careful," said Cass. "I mean, it's kind of dangerous hanging out with somebody who's in the Midnight Sun, don't you think?"

"I was not hanging out with her!" said Yo-Yoji, clenching his fists in frustration.

Max-Ernest tried again. "Guys! Can you stop talking for a second?"

Cass and Yo-Yoji looked at him in surprise. The idea of Max-Ernest, of all people, telling anybody to stop talking was a bit funny, to say the least.

"We're late," he said.

"I know – stop dawdling," said Cass, a little smile

crossing her lips. She started walking. "C'mon, it took us thirty-five minutes to get there last time."

"Thirty-six," Max-Ernest corrected.

Yo-Yoji followed, scowling.

"Bogus," he muttered. "So bogus, it's *re-bog-ulous*."

Although officially an "old-fashioned travelling circus", Pietro's circus hadn't travelled so much as a centimetre in the past year. The half dozen or so tents and equal number of trailers that made up the circus sat on a big dirt lot that by now had come to seem a permanent, if not always pleasant, home to the circus folk.

The lot was surrounded on all sides by an old wire fence. There was only one way in – a dirt road crossed by a rusting chain. Usually, the chain wasn't any real hindrance to passage. You simply walked over it. Or unhooked it from a post if you were driving a car or carting something heavy.

Tonight, there was an additional obstacle blocking their way:

"Who's that?" whispered Cass.

A man – or the shadow of a man – stood stiffly in front of the chain. His arms and legs were spread, signalling that they were not to cross. His face they couldn't see.

He didn't move as they came closer. He could have been a scarecrow.

It didn't necessarily look like the mummy. Then again, in the video, they hadn't been able to see the mummy's face, either.

"Chill," said Yo-Yoji. "Even if there's some mummy walking around out there who wants to kill us for taking his finger, how would he know we were coming here?"

"Yo-Yoji's right," said Max-Ernest. "That wouldn't make any sense."

"Well, let's keep going, then," said Cass. She didn't say what she was thinking: that the ring hanging from her neck might be acting as some kind of homing device, attracting the mummy.

They had no choice but to walk right up to him.

The man was wearing a rumpled old suit and a stained fishing hat with a broken pigeon feather stuck in it. His face was smudged with dirt and grease. He might not have been a mummy, but he looked very much as though he'd been dug out of the ground. Not a reassuring sight, by any means.

"Yo, what's up?" said Yo-Yoji nonchalantly. He kept walking as if he had every intention of stepping over the chain and entering the circus.

"Not so fast, buster," said the man in a low rumble. His arm shot out in front of Yo-Yoji. "Password?"

"Password? We come here all the time," said Max-Ernest, trying not to sound nervous. "We're...friends of Pietro's."

"I don't care if you're friends with the queen of England. Nobody enters without the password."

"But nobody told us the password," said Cass. "We didn't even get a hint!"

"Okay, okay, if you would shut your bazoos and stop barbering for a second, I'll give you punks a hint," said the man, softening. *What a bronc is to a cowboy, a train is to a blank.*"

"That's easy," said Max-Ernest. "A cowboy rides a horse. A *conductor* rides a train."

"That's true, but that's not the password. The password is four letters long."

"Well, how about *pass*, then?" Cass asked. "Short for a *passenger* riding a train. But also for *password*. And for *Why don't you let us pass now – this is crazy*."

"Clever," said the man, not moving. "But no go."

"Wait, I know what it is," said Yo-Yoji unexpectedly.

"*Hobo!*" Max-Ernest blurted out, saying the word at the same time as Yo-Yoji.

Yo-Yoji gave him a look.

"Sorry," said Max-Ernest. "I just figured it out and—"

"And you had to say it, I know," said Yo-Yoji. "No worries."

"You guys got it! *Hobo* it is," said the dishevelled crossing guard. "Just like me." The hobo held up his arms and turned in a circle to show off his outfit. "You like the suit? I dressed up in case anybody saw me leaving those chalk marks today."

"Owen!" cried Cass.

"The very same," said the actor turned Terces Society spy. Grinning, he took off his fishing hat and bowed. "At your service, m'lady."

"I'm going to kill you!" said Cass. (Although she had great affection for Owen, it infuriated Cass that he always pretended to be somebody he wasn't – even when it wasn't strictly necessary.)

"You know who we are – it's not like *we're* in disguises," said Max-Ernest. "Why couldn't you just let us in?"

"What fun would that be? Besides, I'm trying to delay going to the meeting," said Owen, his grin fading.

"Why? What's the meeting about?" asked Yo-Yoji. "Can't be worse than what we've been dealing with."

"Let's just say we have an unfriendly guest."

Alarmed, the kids looked at one another. Could the mummy somehow have found his way into the circus after all?

From somewhere in the darkness came the braying of circus animals and the sound of tents flapping in the wind.

A
Midnight Meeting

It would be hard to overstate the shock Cass, Yo-Yoji and Max-Ernest felt when they saw their old nemesis, Dr. L, sitting by the campfire behind Pietro's trailer.

This was the man who had nearly succeeded in sucking out Benjamin Blake's brains through his nostrils and who had later brainwashed the boy into spying on his friends. (Benjamin was now being home-schooled and, thankfully, was doing very well.) The man who had lured Cass and Max-Ernest aboard his boat and then tried to feed them to sharks. The man who'd helped Ms. Mauvais build a secret chocolate plantation on the backs of slave children. The man they'd last seen dressed as a Renaissance courtier casually orchestrating a lopsided duel between Yo-Yoji and the deadly Lord Pharaoh.

He was one of the leaders of the Midnight Sun. Their sworn enemy. And there he was, sitting on a lawn chair next to Pietro and the other members of the Terces Society, exactly as if he were one of them.

"Peanuts?" Dr. L offered, holding up a striped bag of the classic circus snack. "They are so much better in the shell. I'd forgotten."

Pietro smiled. "My brother and I, we used to climb up the trapeze and throw the peanuts at the clowns," said Pietro, his Italian accent noticeably stronger

– and warmer – than his brother's. "We laughed and laughed, but then we were always too scared to climb back down, *ti ricordi*, Luciano?"

Dr. L chuckled. "That's because the clowns were waiting to throw us into the water with the seals."

The sight of these two men – one looking very much like a man in his seventies or eighties, the other looking half that age – reminiscing together would have been odd even if you didn't know about the intense animosity between them. Under the circumstances, it was unspeakably weird.

The newcomers scanned the faces of the older Terces members for an explanation. From the looks of it, everyone else was as puzzled as they were.

Mr. Wallace, the certified public accountant who was secretly the Terces Society's archivist and oldest surviving member, had a contorted, almost pained expression, as if he were lifting a heavy object (or was just very constipated).

Lily, the violin instructor who happened to be the Terces Society's resident physical-defence expert, stared angrily into the distance, so infuriated by the presence of Dr. L that she couldn't even get herself to nod in welcome to her old student, Yo-Yoji.

Myrtle, the circus's bearded lady and Pietro's gal Friday, stood nearby, grimacing with disapproval.

Owen, meanwhile, kept standing up and sitting down and standing up again, as if he were barely able to keep himself from walking over to the interloper and clobbering him.

Only Pietro seemed happy. He beamed like a proud parent. Gesturing to the three available hay bales, he said, "Take a seat, my young friends. Myrtle, can you make them some hot cocoa?"

Muttering to herself, Myrtle disappeared into the camper.

Dr. L glanced around the circle. "This is all of you? You were stronger in my imagination. I fear my visit here may be in vain."

Owen stood up again, his face red and his fist curled. "We are as strong as we need to be. Strong enough to crush you!"

"Owen, the actor, am I right?" Dr. L inquired. "You certainly have a flair for the dramatic."

"I also have a flair for slugging people in the eye!"

Pietro motioned for Owen to sit. "Please. My brother, he has come to us of his own free will, at great risk to himself. We should listen to what he has to say."

"With all due respect, Pietro, you are blinded by your love," said Mr. Wallace. "What can this man possibly have to say to us?"

"Lies and more lies," Lily spat out. "That's what."

She swatted the ground with her violin bow. As the rest of them knew, the bow was secretly a sword. Lily appeared to be on the verge of using it on Dr. L.

"Anyone else care to share their feelings?" asked Dr. L politely.

Nobody said anything. Their silence was eloquent enough.

"Very well." He smiled thinly. "As you all know, I am not a sentimental man. I do not shudder to see a baby bird taken from its nest. I do not flinch at the sight of blood."

"On the contrary. You take great pleasure in it," said Lily through gritted teeth.

"Not pleasure. Merely interest. I am a scientist. But I am still a man. Somewhere inside."

"You are a little boy inside – that is what you are, *fratello mio*," said Pietro, his old voice trembling with emotion. "The little boy whose childhood, it was stolen from him by that despicable woman, Ms. Mauvais."

Lily swatted the ground with her bow again, her rage reaching the boiling point. "*His* childhood? What about all the childhoods *he* stole?"

Dr. L shrugged. "Perhaps I am still that boy. Or perhaps I was born old... Either way, I have discovered that even I have limits. No longer will I condone the unnecessary loss of life."

"Tell us why you are here," said Pietro gently.

"Well, this is an appropriate location because what I have to say concerns a ghost," said Dr. L, his eyes blazing in the firelight. "The ghost of a Swiss doctor who lived five hundred years ago. The greatest alchemist of his time. Perhaps of all time."

"You mean the rottenest alchemist," said Max-Ernest, taking a cup of hot cocoa from Myrtle, who had just returned. He sipped greedily. The taste of chocolate gave him the courage to address Dr. L without fear. "You're talking about the founder of the Midnight Sun, Lord Pharaoh."

"That is the name he gives himself, yes. He has more than a touch of grandiosity."

"We know all about him – just ask him," said Cass, taking her cup. "And tell him to give me back my monocle."

"I don't think he cares much about that monocle now. You have something he considers much more precious – another band of gold, this one going back to ancient Egypt."

"I don't know what you're talking about," said Cass coolly, doing her best not to call attention to the band of gold hanging from a chain under her shirt.

"It's okay," said Pietro. "He knows you have it."

"Don't forget, Lord Pharaoh was alive when the Jester left it for you, Cassandra," said Dr. L. "The Ring of Thoth is one of the reasons he travelled to the present."

The Ring of Thoth, Cass thought. So that's what it's called. But what is its power?

"Why are you telling us this?" asked Owen suspiciously.

"To warn you." Dr. L looked at Cass. "As long as you have the Ring of Thoth, you are in danger. Lord Pharaoh will stop at nothing to get what he wants."

"Like Ms. Mauvais sending a girl from my school to ask me for it? I think I can handle that."

"Next time, I'll wager, he'll come himself," said Dr. L.

"Does this have anything to do with the missing mummy?" asked Yo-Yoji.

Dr. L shook his head. "I am just as much in the dark as you are about that. But if Cass gives me the ring, I daresay the Midnight Sun will help with that little pickle you're in with the museum. My organization has been known to have some influence."

"We don't want your help!" said Cass, her eyes flashing.

Max-Ernest, uncharacteristically quiet, studied Dr. L. In his readings about card games, Max-Ernest had read about *tells* – those little nervous habits that tell us when someone is bluffing.* He didn't know Dr. L well enough to know what his tell was. Nevertheless, Max-Ernest couldn't help noticing the way the otherwise perfectly composed man was fidgeting with his gloved hands.

As Max-Ernest watched, a small red stain developed on Dr. L's left glove. Blood.

"Think about it," Dr. L urged. "If Lord Pharaoh gets what he wants, you won't have to worry about the mummy again. If not, I fear the mummy will be the least of your worries."

"You sound pretty sure about this," Yo-Yoji interjected. "You sure you don't know where the mummy is?"

"I'm afraid not."

And then Max-Ernest noticed something truly telling: the glove finger above the bloodstain was flopping, loose. In a flash, Max-Ernest knew why.

---

*MY TELL, IN CASE YOU'RE WONDERING, IS A SLIGHT TWITCH IN MY RIGHT EYE, BUT I KNOW BETTER THAN TO LET ANYONE SEE IT. HENCE MY PROPENSITY FOR DARK SUNGLASSES. OF COURSE, EVEN IF I WERE TO TAKE OFF MY SUNGLASSES, YOU WOULDN'T BE ABLE TO TELL WHETHER I WAS TELLING THE TRUTH ABOUT MY TELL. IF MY EYE DIDN'T TWITCH, IT MIGHT MEAN THAT I WAS TELLING THE TRUTH; THEN AGAIN, IT MIGHT MEAN THAT I WAS LYING, AND MY TELL WAS SOMETHING ELSE – WHETHER A FLARING NOSTRIL OR A TAPPING FOOT. YET IF MY EYE TWITCHED, IT WOULD BE EVEN MORE CONFUSING.

"What happened to your hand?" he asked, staring Dr. L in the eye.

"Oh, nothing, a little accident," said Dr. L lightly.

"Can we see?"

"Whatever for? You know how we of the Midnight Sun are about showing our hands. They aren't our best feature."

"So then you admit you're still a member!" said Cass.

"I admit nothing."

"Fine, but you say you're here to help us, right?" observed Max-Ernest. "If you want us to believe you, you should show us your hand as a gesture of good faith."

"Fair enough."

Dr. L started to pull the glove off his right hand.

"No, your left hand."

"Of course."

Dr. L pulled off the left glove and held up his hand for inspection. It was gnarled and veiny and showed all the signs of age that were absent from his smooth and handsome face. Worm-pale from lack of sun, the skin was spotty, scabby, scarred. The yellowed fingernails were cracked and crooked. It was as though his hand had aged ten years for every one that Dr. L had lived. The hand looked so old it could almost have been the hand of a mummy.

Most alarming of all, Dr. L's index finger was missing, a bloody bandage in its place.

"It's just what I thought – he's lying!" exclaimed Max-Ernest, spitting out a mouthful of hot cocoa in his excitement. "Lord Pharaoh has the mummy."

"Why do you say that?" asked Mr. Wallace, staring like everyone else at Dr. L's hand.

"Because he used Dr. L's finger to replace the one I broke off," said Cass, catching on.

"That's why nobody else was on the video," said Max-Ernest. "If a ghost went in to get the mummy, it wouldn't look like anyone else was there. How 'bout that?"

"And then Lord Pharaoh just walked out holding the mummy," said Yo-Yoji, putting it all together. "Like this – so it looked like the mummy was walking." He demonstrated, holding up his hands as if he were gripping the mummy's shoulders.

Pietro's face went cold. "Luciano, is this true?"

"There's no use denying it," said Dr. L. "It was my bad luck that my finger was the closest in size to the mummy's missing finger. Sadly for Lord Pharaoh, it didn't quite take. I fear he will have to find the original."

"Get out of here now," said Pietro, all traces of joy drained from his eyes. "You have lied to me for the last time."

"That's as you wish," said Dr. L, standing. "But let me say this: I lied for a reason. If Cass knew Lord Pharaoh had the mummy, she would never give me the ring. Even if it was the best thing for her. For all of you."

Cass nodded. Dr. L was definitely right about that. Not that she would have given him the ring in any case.

"Everything else I said was true," said Dr. L. "I came here of my own accord to spare you if I could. I see now that that was naive. When Lord Pharaoh gets his hands on the Ring of Thoth – and mark my words, he will get his hands on it – he will be unstoppable. You have no idea what you're up against."

"We'll take our chances," said Owen.

"You see, Lord Pharaoh believes he really is a pharaoh, and therefore, like a pharaoh, he should be a god on earth," Dr. L continued sombrely. "The Ring of Thoth is the key. When it is reunited with the mummy, the Secret will be revealed."

Cass fancied she felt the ring buzzing against her chest, but she tried to ignore it.

"After Lord Pharaoh learns the Secret, he will be immortal. And all-powerful. He will claim any body he desires as his own – whether the mummy's or one of ours – and he will walk the earth in our clothes like a living god. The whole world will do his bidding."

As Dr. L pronounced these words, a breeze suddenly passed over them, and the flames of the campfire briefly flickered out, much as if they'd been squelched by a ghost.

The group momentarily fell silent, everyone staring nervously into the darkness. But if Lord Pharaoh was there, he showed no further sign.

"As I see it, you have two options," said Dr. L, looking at Cass. "You can give me the ring now and hope Lord Pharaoh forgets about you—"

"Never," said Cass.

"Or you can try to beat him at his own game."

"You mean put the ring on the mummy before he does?" asked Yo-Yoji, incredulous.

"That's right. If you restore the mummy's finger and you put the ring on him, then you, not Lord Pharaoh, will learn the Secret."

"But, uh, as we established earlier, Lord Pharaoh has the mummy, not us," said Max-Ernest. "We don't even have the finger. And even if we did, how would we put it back on?"

"At the risk of repeating a cliché, I didn't say it would be easy."

Dr. L turned to his brother. "*Prego*, a parting gift."

Before Pietro could protest, Dr. L handed him a small glass vial with what looked like a drop of oil and a dry flower petal at the bottom. MANDOLIN–ROSE read the old, faded label on the side. The label was charred around the edges; the vial had survived a fire.

"That little bottle is all that remains of our Symphony of Smells. Guard it well," said Dr. L softly. *"Arrivederci, fratello mio."*

With those parting words, Dr. L bowed curtly to the assembled members of the Terces Society and walked out into the night.

As the grief-stricken Pietro opened the vial from the Symphony of Smells and inhaled the scent, the other adult Terces members argued about how best to respond to what Dr. L had told them. What part was true? What part a lie? Could Dr. L be trusted at all?

The three younger members, meanwhile, stared into the fire, contemplating the days ahead. Each was thinking the same thing: that they had little choice but to follow Dr. L's advice. Pietro might not insist that they go on such a foolhardy and dangerous adventure. He might not even allow it. But for them, the mission was as clear as if it had been written on a chalkboard:

1. RETRIEVE MUMMY'S FINGER.
2. PUT FINGER BACK ON MUMMY.
3. PUT RING BACK ON FINGER.
4. LEARN THE SECRET.

And...

5. PRAY THEY WEREN'T FALLING INTO A TRAP.

An Exam

NOTE: From time to time, readers ask me if they can join the Terces Society. My responses to this request are many and various, but usually they amount to the same thing:

No.

As in, *No, you aren't even supposed to know about the Terces Society in the first place.*

As in, *No, it's not exactly a joining kind of thing – you have to be asked.*

As in, *No, I couldn't even tell you if we were going to ask you.*

As in, *No, what makes you think I have any pull with the Terces Society after writing these horribly irresponsible books?*

However, it's always good to be prepared. Or so I hear.

Below you will find an example of the kind of arduous and probing mental examination you should expect should a certain unnamed secret society deem you worthy of its members' attention. Please destroy this document after completion. Your discretion is appreciated.

– PB

TERCES SOCIETY
PRACTICE PRE-ENTRANCE EXAM

1. Name:_____

2. Alias/pseudonym:_____

3. The Terces Society is
   a) a club dedicated to the study and appreciation
      of dung beetles.
   b) a secret organization devoted to the protection
      of an ancient and powerful secret.
   c) an odd group of hieroglyph enthusiasts.
   d) none of your business, buster.
   e) the what society? Sorry, never heard of it.

**4. The Secret Series by Pseudonymous Bosch is
best avoided because**
   a) it refers to a secret that makes people go mad
      with curiosity and will most likely have the
      same effect on you.
   b) if you like chocolate, the books will make you
      hungry and jealous of all the chocolate the
      author eats; if you don't like chocolate, you
      won't like the books.

5. If you were an animal, you would be a

a) sloth.

b) giraffe.

c) panda.

d) larval insect.

e) You already are an animal.

6. Given the choice, you would

a) lead an exciting life full of danger and adventure.

b) lead a quiet and contemplative life.

c) eat a lot of chocolate.

7. True or false?

I would never reveal the Secret for any price.

8. Essay question:

Chocolate is to cheese as chess is to checkers. Explain.

_____

_____

_____

_____

_____

_____

_____

ANSWERS

Use the answers below to score your exam. Award one point for every correct answer. Any score above eight points out of a possible seven is considered a passing score. (Hint: although cheating is frowned upon, it is acceptable to award yourself bonus points for particularly good answers.)

1. The correct answer is blank. As a member of the Terces Society, you should never volunteer your name.
2. Thank you. That's more like it.
3. e).
4. Both, of course.
5. There is no correct answer; it is a subjective question.
   Correction: as my rabbit, Quiche, would hasten to tell you, the *correct* answer is e). You are an animal – because we humans are all animals.
6. I hope I don't have to supply the answer to this one!
7. False. *I* would definitely reveal the Secret for a price – if the price were high enough and involved enough chocolate. What *you* would do – that's another question.
8. Actually, this question is not really on the exam. But I'm very interested to hear what you have to say on the topic.

The Heist
Part One

The next morning, Cass made a solemn confession to her mother: *she* wanted to return the mummy, she said, but her friends refused to admit they'd taken it. (Technically, you might notice, this was true. She *did* want to return the mummy – unfortunately, she didn't have it. Likewise, her friends *did* refuse to admit they'd taken the mummy – because, in fact, they hadn't.) She told her mom that she was going to spend time with Max-Ernest and Yo-Yoji after school in order to try to persuade them to do the right thing.

Max-Ernest and Yo-Yoji told *their* parents more or less the same thing – i.e., that *they* wanted to return the mummy but that *their* friends refused to admit they'd taken it.

The story was that they would be working on their graduation speeches at the public library. They were packing snacks, and they wouldn't be home until dinner time. The time frame was optimistic – there was a very good chance they wouldn't be home until late that night, or maybe ever – but they figured that was the latest hour they could name without further explanation.

As soon as they got to the library, they went into their respective bathrooms to change. Cass was the last to come out, tugging on her dress so it would stay where it was supposed to.

That's right: her dress.

Let that sink in for a moment: Cass. In. A. Dress.

And did I mention she was wearing lipstick? Pink lipstick.

Had she lost her mind? Undergone a religious conversion?

Actually, she was in disguise. All three of them had adopted disguises of one sort or another. They weren't exactly expecting to see WANTED posters with their photographs hanging on every wall of the museum, but they figured the disguises might buy them some time should they be spotted by Albert 3-D or one of the security personnel they'd met previously. Also, the disguises might help keep them from being recognized if they were caught on a surveillance video again.

Not *would* help. *Might* help.

"Don't say anything," said Cass before either of her friends could speak. "I know, I look ridiculous. I mean *ridiculous* ridiculous. My mom bought me the dress for graduation, but no way am I wearing it then –"

"It's…nice," said Yo-Yoji.

"Yeah, nice," agreed Max-Ernest, although he wasn't sure whether Yo-Yoji had meant nice as in *you look nice*, or nice as in *nice disguise*, or nice as in *not nice at all*.

"Just don't let anybody see your fingernails," said Yo-Yoji, snickering. "They kinda give you away."

Her ears reddening, Cass glanced at her nails for a second. Yo-Yoji was right; they still looked raw and ragged from all the chewing, not very girlish at all.

"Well, at least I don't look like some kind of hipster-raver clown," she said, hiding her fingernails in her fist.

Max-Ernest snorted. Yo-Yoji had simply dressed in one of his everyday outfits, which today consisted of neon-yellow sneakers, skinny black jeans, an acid-green T-shirt, and an orange baseball cap on top of his blue-streaked hair – not exactly inconspicuous. The only additions to his everyday attire: a pair of 1950s Wayfarer-style sunglasses and a camera around his neck.

"You just don't get it," said Yo-Yoji. "I'm dressed as a Japanese tourist."

"You *are* a Japanese tourist," Max-Ernest pointed out.

"Yeah, but not that kind," said Yo-Yoji. "It's like if you dressed as a nerd on purpose."

"What do you mean?"

"Well, you're a nerd, right? But you're cool."

"I am?!" Max-Ernest couldn't have been more surprised if Yo-Yoji had told him he had sprouted antlers.

"Well, not *that* cool," Yo-Yoji amended. "I mean,

you're not like one of those cool nerds – that's a whole other thing."

Max-Ernest had employed the props at his disposal: a pair of wire-frame eyeglasses and a fake moustache. They were left over from the Halloween when he'd dressed as Sherlock Holmes's partner, Dr. Watson. (Cass had vetoed his original costume, Sherlock Holmes, on the basis that Max-Ernest shouldn't promote something as carcinogenic as pipe smoking.) The moustache wasn't quite as preposterous-looking as you might imagine; it matched his hair colour and wasn't overly bushy.

To their credit, Cass and Yo-Yoji refrained from making fun of him. Almost.

"You're supposed to be a midget, right?" asked Yo-Yoji. "Like, from the circus?"

"That's rude," Cass admonished. "They're called *little people*, remember?"

After enduring a few more jibes, Max-Ernest peeled off the moustache. But he kept the glasses.

"That's better," said Yo-Yoji. "Now you're going for nerdy nerd."

Max-Ernest nodded, uncertain whether this was a compliment.

As luck would have it (actually, there was nothing lucky about it; they had planned it that way), the public library was only a block away from their real destination – the Natural History Museum. Specifically, the Restoration Room, where they hoped to find the mummy's finger still sitting in a shoebox high on a shelf, squeezed between two urns.

They stopped just before they reached the museum's front steps.

Yo-Yoji squinted under his sunglasses. "Who are those dudes?"

Across the street stood three men in white turbans and robes. They shook bells and tambourines and held handmade signs, like protestors at a political event.

THE MUMMY RISES

FREE AMUN NOW!

THE PRIESTS OF AMUN ARE WATCHING

Max-Ernest frowned. "How can Amun be freed? He's a mummy. Plus, he's already broken out."

"Come on, guys," said Cass. "Forget about them – they're just some wacky cult. It's time to go steal a finger."

★　★　★

The first time they'd visited the museum, they were on a field trip. The second time, they were working there. Neither time had they paid admission, and it was something of a shock to find themselves lining up at the front desk to buy tickets.

The price of three student tickets: eighteen dollars.

What they had between them: nine dollars and thirty-five cents.

"I could try paying with gold," said Cass. She had stashed a few of the Jester's gold coins in the bottom of her backpack for emergencies.*

"It's okay. We can pay what we want," said Max-Ernest, scrutinizing the writing above the desk. "Look – *recommended donation*. How 'bout that?"

As it turned out, Max-Ernest was correct, although the man selling tickets was decidedly unhappy about it. "Don't come back," he said under his breath as he took one dollar for the three tickets.

The museum didn't close until five p.m. That meant they had an hour and a half to kill, exploring the museum and trying their best to blend in with ordinary visitors.

---

*IN THE EVENT OF ALL-OUT NUCLEAR WAR OR SOME OTHER KIND OF GLOBAL DISASTER, PAPER MONEY WOULD PROBABLY BE WORTHLESS, CASS THOUGHT; GOLD WAS MORE LIKELY TO MAINTAIN ITS VALUE.

They lingered the longest in the Rocks and Minerals Room. It was the darkest part of the museum – the better to show off the crystals and geodes under the spotlights – and they figured it was where they were least likely to be recognized or caught on camera. As a side benefit, Cass was able to compare the gems in the show with the raw gems she'd found in the Jester's trunk. (She determined that her gems were most likely garnets and not, as she'd first thought, rubies.)

As they walked around, they discussed where to hide at closing time. This would be the most treacherous moment in their day, when they were most likely to be herded out with the other malingerers or, worse, identified as thieves planning to purloin an ancient artefact from the museum.

Their first thought, inspired by a certain book they'd all read, was to hide in a bathroom, standing on toilets in case somebody looked under the stall doors. But experience at school had taught them that there was a good chance the janitors might start cleaning the toilets immediately after the museum closed. (And if they weren't clean, then...yuck.) They decided against bathrooms. Likewise they decided against trash cans (none were big enough to hide inside) and animal dioramas (all were locked).

Finally, they settled on the spot they knew best. It meant returning to the mummy exhibit. And it would be snug for the three of them, to say the least. But who would look there? After all, it was already known to be empty. The Priests of Amun notwithstanding, a mummy rising from the dead is generally a one-time-only event.

On reflection, Dr. Amun's sarcophagus was the perfect hiding place.

At exactly five minutes before five, after they'd all availed themselves of their last opportunity to use a bathroom, they entered the mummy exhibit for what they expected would be the last time. It was the last hour of the last day of the show, and the gallery was extremely crowded. This was a good thing and a bad thing: good because they were immediately camouflaged by the multitude of museum visitors, bad because there was no way to slip into the mummy's chamber without being seen.

Unlike the cost of the tickets, the crowd problem hadn't caught our young aspiring museum robbers by surprise. A diversion was called for, and they were expert at creating diversions. It hadn't been long, after all, since Max-Ernest had staged an epileptic fit so masterfully authentic that it brought a hospital emergency room to a halt.

Cass nodded discreetly in the direction of the security guard watching over the mummy exhibit. The guard was somebody they'd seen before but had never met. There was a decent chance she would recognize them, and it was risky to interact with her, but they had no choice if they were to proceed with their plan. They needed to get her out of the room and then to draw the crowd's attention away from the mummy's chamber long enough for them to sneak into the chamber and lie down in the sarcophagus. About one and a half minutes in all, they estimated.

Yo-Yoji and Max-Ernest nodded back. The plan was a go.

Max-Ernest looked at his watch, then started counting down with his fingers. Three . . . two . . . one . . . time to move.

As the three friends separated, taking their respective positions across the mummy exhibit's main room, they held their breath. They weren't entirely inexperienced when it came to criminal activity. As you may recall, in the course of their past adventures, they'd been forced to acquire certain necessary objects through, let's say, *creative* methods. Nonetheless, they'd never robbed a museum before, and they couldn't help feeling more than a little anxiety about the job ahead. A museum robbery is the kind of thing you see on the news; you don't necessarily expect to be involved in one yourself. The fact that they intended to return the mummy's finger later, reattached to the missing mummy, might or might not have justified their actions on a moral level, but it didn't make what they were doing any less terrifying.

Their plan had two parts:

First, Yo-Yoji uncapped a water bottle and stealthily emptied it next to his foot, creating a large puddle on the marble floor. Before anybody noticed the puddle, he walked quickly to the animal section of the exhibit and pretended to examine a display of a mummified cat. Only after staring at the display for a moment did he realize that the cat was missing; all the animal mummies had been packed in crates that were lined up against the wall in preparation for the exhibit's move to Las Vegas. He glanced around – happily, nobody had seen his mistake.

Meanwhile, Cass, the most fully disguised of the three of them – and, hopefully, the hardest to recognize – ran up to the guard.

"Excuse me, ma'am," Cass said in a polite but urgent voice. "Somebody spilled water over there."

She pointed across the room to the spill, just visible between the legs of museum-goers.

The guard shrugged. "The show closes in five minutes."

"Yes, and that's more than enough time for somebody to slip," said Cass firmly.

"I guess you're right." Giving Cass an evil look, the guard sighed and reached for her walkie-talkie.

Uh-oh, thought Cass. Instead of leaving the room, the guard was going to call for help. Thinking fast, Cass shook her head. "You'd better go get a mop right now. It could take for ever for a janitor to get here. In the meantime, any of those people could fall and fracture a wrist, or even suffer a traumatic head injury."

The guard hesitated, not wanting to leave her post.

"Think about the lawsuits – you could lose your job," urged Cass. "Go, go, there's not a second to lose!"

Now seriously worried, the guard nodded and ran off.

As Cass breathed a sigh of relief, Max-Ernest was initiating phase two of their plan: the stink bomb.

As happens occasionally when you take care of a baby for long stretches of time, Max-Ernest had earlier that afternoon found a full diaper balled up inside his backpack. He'd been about to drop it into a trash can, when Cass stopped him. They might have use for something smelly later.

It worked beautifully. The diaper had been festering in a ziplock bag for several days, and when Max-Ernest opened the bag, he could almost feel the smell slapping him in the face. People started looking around nervously, wondering who or what had caused the terrible stench. As the smell filled the room, visitors filed out as fast as they could.

There was a momentary scare when, as Cass had warned might happen, somebody slipped on the wet marble. Luckily, it was a young man, who quickly regained his balance and walked out with nothing bruised but his ego.

Cass, Max-Ernest and Yo-Yoji held their noses until the last person had left the room. Then Max-Ernest hastily closed the ziplock bag and tossed it into a waste bin. (He had no intention of using it as a stink bomb a second time.)

Wordlessly, the three friends darted over to the mummy's chamber and let themselves in.

Because the sarcophagus had been built to hold a coffin, which in turn had been built to hold another coffin, which in turn had been built to hold another coffin, the container was quite large. The bottom of the sarcophagus was covered with a layer of sand, however, and they had to shift around a bit to get down far enough to feel safe from detection. It was a difficult operation for three people to perform at once.

Without thinking about it, they fell into their usual formation from the school bus, with Yo-Yoji stretched out on one side and Max-Ernest and Cass scrunched up on the other. It wasn't the most comfortable hiding place in the world, but not terrible. Considering.

"So far so good," whispered Max-Ernest.

"Yeah, nice job, dudes," said Yo-Yoji.

Cass put her finger to her lips; it wasn't over yet. But she allowed herself a small smile of victory.

And there they lay, like three squirming mummies awaiting their burial.

The Heist
Part Two

Hiding in the sarcophagus, they could hear somebody cleaning up Yo-Yoji's spill. It seemed to take an awfully long time, but finally they heard the sound of a mop being dropped into a pail and then heavy footsteps leaving the room. After waiting an additional three minutes to be safe, Yo-Yoji stuck his head out and gave the all clear.

With sand pouring off their clothes, they climbed out of the sarcophagus and glanced nervously around Dr. Amun's chamber and out into the exhibit area beyond. They knew they were being filmed, so they covered their faces with their hands as they made their way out of the chamber. Anybody watching the video later was likely to recognize them, but they hoped that with their disguises and their covered faces, they might plausibly deny they were there.

The stairs leading down to the Restoration Room were only a few dozen feet away, but it felt like they were crossing a football field. Or, perhaps more aptly, a graveyard. They could almost feel the mummies' eyes on them as they passed. Twice they heard voices coming from other parts of the museum, but they made it through without being interrupted by anybody, dead or alive.

* * *

They stopped at the bottom of the stairwell, where there was a door marked EMPLOYEES ONLY.

When they'd last passed through it, they'd practically been employees themselves, accompanied by a senior curator of the museum. This time, they approached the door with considerably more trepidation. Now they were thieves in the midst of a heist, even if the only thing they planned to steal was a severed finger, which they meant to return soon.

Above the door handle was a keypad-style lock. Albert 3-D had explained that the five-letter pass code changed weekly. "Or when I can remember to change it," he'd told them with a self-deprecating smile.

Rather than informing the other staff every time he changed the code, he always left clues on the door. It was sort of a game. A twig, for example, might mean the code was STICK. A piece of tape might mean STUCK. (Then again, I suppose, it might mean STICK, too – in the sense of *sticky*.)

Today, two images were pasted above the lock. The first was an image taken from an Egyptian tomb painting: a falcon-headed man standing under a large disc. The second was a child's sticker: a cartoon image of a school bus.

Cass looked at Max-Ernest. "Well?"

There was no question that figuring out the pass

code was his department. The question, her tone conveyed, was whether he could figure it out before they were caught red-handed by a security guard.

"The first one is easy," said Max-Ernest. "That's the sun god, Ra. You can tell by the disc over his head – it represents the sun. I'm not sure what the school bus means. Maybe just *school*? Which would give us RA SCHOOL as the clue…"

"What about RASCAL?" asked Yo-Yoji. "I like that word."

Max-Ernest shook his head. "Has to be five letters, remember? That's six."

"Just RA BUS, then?" suggested Cass.

"I doubt it – too random," said Max-Ernest. He tried the words anyway, but the light remained red.

Cass was bouncing on her feet with impatience. "So what is it, then?"

"I don't know. Just give me a – oh no," said Max-Ernest, turning pale. "It can't be…"

"What? Tell us already," said Cass.

"Yeah, you're scaring us, man," said Yo-Yoji.

"Not RA…BUS…" Max-Ernest said slowly. "ROB… US…"

They all looked at one another. The implication was scary: they were expected.

"No way," said Yo-Yoji. "How would he know?"

His hand shaking slightly, Max-Ernest tried the password. It didn't work.

They all exhaled in relief. The robbery wasn't anticipated after all.

"We still have to get in," said Cass. "If we stand here for ever—"

"I know, I know. Let me think," said Max-Ernest. "Without the disc on top, the god would be called Horus...but I don't think that helps. Sometimes RA is spelled RE, with an *E*."

"RE BUS, maybe? Does RE stand for any kind of bus?" asked Yo-Yoji. "You know, like the name of a bus line?"

"No, but you just got it anyway," said Max-Ernest, starting to giggle. "REBUS – I can't believe I didn't think of it right away. It's hilarious."

His friends looked at him quizzically. By now, Max-Ernest was about to fall down laughing.

"Don't you get it? The rebus is REBUS!"

They shook their heads. They didn't get it. And they didn't get *him*, either.

"A rebus is a kind of code in which pictures or words equal sounds. Like *Ra* and *bus* for ROB US, even though that wasn't right. Or, like, if you saw a drawing of an eye – it could mean an eye you see with, but it could also mean the sound of the word. You know how people will draw an eye and then a heart and then the letter *U* – and it means *I love you*?"

Cass made a face. "Gross."

Max-Ernest blushed. "I wasn't saying—"

Cass laughed. "I know. Aren't *I* ever allowed to make a joke?"

"Oh, I mean, yes," said Max-Ernest, relieved. "Anyway, it figures that Albert 3-D would be into rebuses because hieroglyphs work like that, with pictures for sounds."

"Come on, let's go snag the mummy's finger and then bail," said Yo-Yoji, looking over his shoulder to make sure they were still alone. "This is getting—"

"*Rebus-ulous?*" finished Max-Ernest, cracking himself up again.

He punched the word into the keypad. The light turned green.

They made it all the way to the Restoration Room without hearing or seeing anybody aside from the sewn and stuffed and reassembled residents of the Osteology and Taxidermy Room. Of course, they'd been hoping not to meet anybody, but there was something eerie about it, nonetheless.

"I feel like at any second people are going to jump out and yell 'Surprise!'" said Cass.

"Yeah, only instead of singing 'Happy Birthday', they're going to arrest us," said Max-Ernest.

"Way to think positive," said Yo-Yoji. "Look, it's right there. Everything's copacetic."

He pointed to the shelf. The shoebox in which Albert 3-D kept the mummy's finger was exactly where they remembered it being placed, between the urns. Using the bottom shelf as a step, Cass reached up and took it down.

All three of them looked inside simultaneously – and simultaneously their three faces fell.

"What the—?!" exclaimed Yo-Yoji.

"Is that what I think it is?" asked Max-Ernest.

"Uh-huh," said Cass bleakly.

There was something lying on the linen inside the box, but it wasn't the mummy's finger. It wasn't anybody's finger.

It was a gold-framed monocle. The Double Monocle. The monocle that Lord Pharaoh had taken from Cass when they'd tussled months earlier. Somebody – no doubt, Lord Pharaoh – had removed the mummy's finger from the box and left the monocle in the finger's place.

"He's sending us a message," said Yo-Yoji.

"Yeah, that he's one step ahead of us," said Max-Ernest.

"Watching us..." said Cass, looking over her shoulder.

Remembering the unique powers of the monocle, Cass put it to her eye and looked around the room. With the monocle she could see around corners and even through a few walls, but she didn't see Lord Pharaoh or any other ghosts – only Albert 3-D entering through the employee exit.

"C'mon, we gotta go!" she whispered, replacing the shoebox on the shelf (minus the monocle). "Albert's coming!"

It was a lucky break she'd tried the monocle when she did: one more minute and Albert 3-D would have caught them with the shoebox in their hands. But where to go? They'd been planning on leaving through the employee exit, but if they went that way, they would run directly into him.

"Back that way!" Cass pointed at the door to the Osteology and Taxidermy Room.

Trying not to make any noise, they raced out of the Restoration Room just before Albert 3-D entered it. They could hear him following behind them, speaking to a colleague.

"We're just going to have to set up in Vegas as planned and hope we get the mummy back. The Cairo Hotel is not going to be happy, but what else can we do?"

Alas, the footsteps didn't stop. Albert 3-D was headed in their direction.

"Upstairs," said Yo-Yoji. The others nodded; they had no choice.

When they got to the top of the stairs, the door below started to open. There would be no time to get out of the exhibit area before Albert 3-D entered it.

"Quick – the sarcophagus!" whispered Cass.

"No, that's probably where they're going," whispered Yo-Yoji. "What about those crates in there?" He nodded in the direction of the packed-up animal mummies.

As fast as they could, they ran to the crates. The crates were various sizes, with stencilled arrows and warnings on their sides. The biggest was roughly the size of a refrigerator. Its back was open. The crate was more than half-full, but there would be just enough space for them if they squeezed.

They crawled inside. Yo-Yoji closed the hinged door just before they heard footsteps in the next room.

In their haste, they had failed to notice that they weren't alone.

Revenge of the
Cat Mummy

They crouched in the darkness, sandwiched between boxes, afraid to speak. Every sound echoed inside the crate. They could hear Albert 3-D and his colleague walking into the exhibit. Then more footsteps. And more footsteps. There must have been four or five people at least, all speaking at once.

"Are all the dead guys going or just the Egyptians?" *"What about these statues – the what do you call 'em? Shoddy figures?"* *"Hey, careful – you don't want to break another finger! We lost one already!"*

Soon the voices gave way to the sounds of banging and prising and hammering. Tools falling on the floor. Workers swearing. The exhibit was being packed up.

Without consulting one another, Cass, Max-Ernest and Yo-Yoji were all asking themselves the same thing: should they give themselves up now and face the wrath of Albert 3-D, their parents and possibly the police? Or should they wait until it was quiet again and hope to escape unseen then? The first option was horrifying but sensible. The second was appealing but unrealistic.

Nobody uttered a whisper. They would wait.

Another minute passed.

Max-Ernest was the first to notice the hulking shadow looming behind them.

He pointed. "Uh—"

Cass clamped her hand down on his mouth.

Max-Ernest pointed again, more vehemently.

His friends peered into the darkness. Only a little bit of light was coming through the cracks in the crate, but their eyes were adjusting.

Had they judged by shape alone, they might have determined that their mysterious companion was a Spanish woman grieving silently under her lace *mantilla*; a wizard sitting asleep under his cloak; or a two-year-old standing under a sheet, dressed as a ghost.

Cass instinctively reached around to get her flashlight, but her backpack was stuck between two boxes. Before she could dislodge it, her phone started vibrating. Cass froze – but luckily she had thought to silence her phone before entering the museum. She looked at the screen. It was her mother calling. Soon the urgent texts would begin.

The light of her phone filled the crate with a soft glow.

Now they could see who was sitting behind them:

A cat mummy.

The layers of bubble wrap surrounding the cat mummy had increased its size to that of a dog and had given it the shape of a pear. They could tell it was a cat, however, because the face of a cat was painted on top of the linen bandages where its real face would have been; and legs and paws were painted to show the cat sitting up tall. All in all, the cat mummy was a relieving sight – better a dead cat than a live witness – but not a very comforting one.

Cass shuddered, and she was glad that her friends couldn't see her.

Yo-Yoji tapped his friends on their legs to get their attention. Then, smiling to himself, he took his Wayfarer sunglasses off his head and put them on the cat mummy.

Cass and Max-Ernest both shook their heads in alarm – what if they damaged another mummy?! – but then they smiled, too. It was the first bit of comic relief they'd had in several hours – make that *days*.

Yo-Yoji pulled out his phone. He typed, then held up the screen for the others to see: **Game . . . Ask a Cat Mummy.**

He gave Cass a nudge – her turn.

She hesitated. It was hardly the time for a game, but suddenly she was feeling punchy. **How long will we be in here?**

Yo-Yoji typed the answer as quickly as he could: **Cat mummy says, until Nile floods or dinner. Whichevr comes 1st.**

Cass rolled her eyes. **Okay, Cat mummy. What is the meaning of life?**

Yo-Yoji didn't miss a beat. **Cat mummy says, u will have no life if albert 3d catches u here.**

But Max-Ernest had his own answer: ***Life* means cellular activity including vital phenomena such as growth, reproduction, digestion.**

Yo-Yoji covered his mouth to keep from laughing. Max-Ernest looked at him in the darkness, confused. Was that funny? Then he resumed typing, correcting himself. **Oh. I mean, Cat mummy says.**

The game continued, the cellphone screens lighting their faces with an eerie glow. To an outside observer, it would have looked as if they were engaged in some kind of electronic séance, attempting to summon the spirit of the cat mummy with their phones. Alas, the cat uttered not a single meow.

The only spooky voice they heard came about five minutes later. It was Albert 3-D's:

"Hey, have any of you guys seen three kids around? Two boys and a girl. Something was stolen and I think they took it."

"What was it?" asked one of the workers.

"Just a finger – this time."

The three kids sat frozen in the crate, only a few metres away from him. Just when they thought things couldn't get any worse, they were being blamed for another one of Lord Pharaoh's crimes!

Cass returned to her phone, fingers flying. **LP couldn't hv planned it better if he wanted to set us up!**

Maybe he did set us up, wrote Max-Ernest. **We should hv known not to listen to dr. L.**

Yo-Yoji held up his phone. **So what now?**

Before either of his friends could answer, they heard a beeping sound. The kind a truck makes when it's backing up. The beeping got louder and louder as they listened, until it sounded as if it were right next to them.

What's that? typed Max-Ernest.

Pickup truck? guessed Cass.

Inside a museum? scoffed Yo-Yoji.

A moment later, they heard the hum of a motor, and they could feel something sliding under the crate. The crate tilted slightly, sending Max-Ernest skidding into Cass.

"Aaak!" Max-Ernest cried out spontaneously.

"You hear that?" It was one of the workers.

"What?"

"I just thought I heard somebody cry out. In here –" He knocked on the side of the crate.

The other man laughed. *"Yeah, a mummy!"*

"Hello, anybody home?" There was more knocking and more laughter. *"Okay, going up..."*

At these words, the kids could feel the crate being lifted in the air. It felt as if they were in an elevator – a very small elevator.

Forklift! typed Yo-Yoji.

Cass looked at her friends. **Should we say something??**

Max-Ernest nodded. **Yeah. Like right now. Time to get out!!**

No! wrote Yo-Yoji. **This is perfect. They'll take us out of the museum. Then we get out and nobody sees us.**

They heard the sound of the forklift being put into gear. And suddenly they were moving forwards.

(If you can call it forward when you're trapped in the darkness with no room to move, headed for an unknown destination, unsure whether you're ever going to get out or if you're going to be inadvertently entombed alongside a cat mummy.)

After a few minutes, they heard a clanking sound: a hook attaching to the crate.

As they clutched their stomachs, fighting nausea, the crate was lifted to what could only have been an extremely dangerous height. It swung left, then right, then up, then down, further down, left again, right again, and right some more.

Crane? Cass typed. Or that's what she meant to write. In actuality, she typed, **oakdgpai upg.**

By the time the crate stopped swinging, Cass had somehow ended up with her foot caught between Max-Ernest's knee and Yo-Yoji's face.

It was a good thing they couldn't see her.

As they disentangled themselves, the three bruised and embarrassed friends heard the clang of a gate closing – and the whine of a diesel motor.

Uh-oh, wrote Max-Ernest.

None of them said anything for a minute as their situation sank in.

Max-Ernest typed into his phone again: **We better text our parents while we still have batteries.**

Yo-Yoji showed his phone to Cass. **u hv supplies, right?**

Cass nodded. **Water and trail mix in backpack. And m-e has chocolate.**

Max-Ernest paled in the darkness. He had just taken a chocolate bar out of his bag. How did she know?

The chocolate is mine!

Cass wrote back: **If u want water, u have to share. Next time, don't crinkle the wrapper, it makes noise.**

Hate you! Max-Ernest responded, breaking off a couple of modestly generous pieces of chocolate for her and Yo-Yoji. (Had he known just how long they were going to be in there, he might have been even stricter about the size of the rations.) Then he settled back and started working on a new draft of his graduation speech.

CHAPTER TWENTY- THREE

The I'm-Never-Going- to-Graduate Graduation Speech

NOTE: The text below was originally written on a cellphone. I have corrected all errors and abbreviations for ease of reading.

GRADUATION SPEECH – THIRD DRAFT

TITLE:
The I'm-Never-Going-to-Graduate Graduation Speech, aka Max-Ernest's Last Will and Testament

JOKE:
What did the cat mummy say to the dog mummy?...
No, wait, I've got it... What is a dog mummy's favourite trick?
Playing dead. (Heh. Good one, Max-Ernest!)

SPEECH:
Most speeches are written to be read aloud, but not this one because (a) I am most likely going to die of suffocation and/or starvation, trapped in a dark crate, and (b) even if I survive this insane adventure, there's no way Mrs. Johnson is going to let me graduate, let alone read a speech. On the plus side, that means I can write whatever I want. So what do I want to write? What's the really mean and terrible thing I've been wanting to say or the huge confession

I've been wanting to make? Hmm, I don't have one, really.

I guess just this — Cass and Yo-Yoji, if I die first, and this phone drops from my cold, dead hands, and you have the bright idea to see if I wrote anything on it, and there's still some battery power left, and you haven't yet gone blind from hunger, I just want to say I'm glad I was with you guys at the end. There's nobody I'd rather play cat mummy with. Or even be mummified with. You're the best friends I ever had. Well, you're the only friends I ever had, but you know what I mean.

CHAPTER
TWENTY-
FOUR

Touchy

Four variations on the word *touch*:

Don't touch Pseudonymous Bosch on the head.

Mr. Bosch is very touchy about his head.

Old Bosch, you could say, is touched in the head.

Ask him for money – Bosch is a soft touch due to soft head.

Poor Bosch! Such a touching story about his head!

Bosch responds (off the top of his head):

Touché!

CHAPTER TWENTY-FIVE

A Bird,
a Scorpion,
and a Baby

Cass awoke in darkness, curled up in a ball and aching all over. She fought the urge to panic. Where was she? Had she been kidnapped? In an accident?

Reflexively, she felt her wrists to see if she'd been tied up. Or had any injuries. No, she was fine.

She sat up – and hit her head.

Oh. The crate. She was still in the crate.

She could hear Max-Ernest and Yo-Yoji snoring. Otherwise, it was strangely quiet. The low hum they had heard for hours and hours was gone. The crate was no longer moving. Wherever they were, they were sitting still.

She clicked her phone on. She was just able to see the time before the battery gave out: six thirty a.m. The morning! They'd slept all night. There was no way to know how far they'd travelled. For all she knew, they could have journeyed halfway around the world. On the other hand, they could be less than a kilometre from the Natural History Museum.

Afraid to make any noise, she felt around for Max-Ernest and Yo-Yoji, then awakened them by shaking a leg and an arm, respectively.

"Huh?"

"Where are—?"

"Shh!" she hissed. "Don't say anything!"

They were groggy and sore, but there was no need to debate next steps. They all wanted to get out. As soon as they could.

The operation was a little more difficult than they'd anticipated. The crate was not meant to carry live human passengers, only dead feline ones, and therefore the door was not designed to be opened from the inside. Using Cass's flashlight, a screwdriver and a toothpick, they had to pick the lock from the back – which is often easier than picking a lock from the front, but it takes some getting used to. It's like reading upside down or tying somebody else's shoes. (I assume you have plenty of experience picking locks the usual way; but for the record, I don't condone reading your best friend's sister's diary, only your own sister's diary.) Eventually, however, the springs and levers gave way, the door swung open, and the crate was flooded with light.

Temporarily blinded, our friends held their breath, hoping there were no unfriendly forces waiting outside, whether museum workers or Midnight Sun members. But nobody attacked them. Nobody yelled at them or expressed shock at seeing them. There were no sounds or movements of any kind.

"Where the heck are we?!" asked Yo-Yoji when his eyes started to adjust.

They peered out the door in astonishment.

* * *

The crate was sitting inside what appeared to be the stone ruins of an ancient Egyptian temple. On either side were walls covered entirely with hieroglyphs so well preserved that they still showed the colours of the original paint. Gods and pharaohs, slaves and children, plants and animals, the whole panoply of Egyptian life was depicted. Directly in front of where the crate sat was a row of thick decorative columns that ended in capitals designed to look like lotus flowers. Beyond the temple, the desert stretched out in all directions, a sea of soft, rippling sand dunes. A perfect yellow sun hovered above a sky that was the same brilliant blue as the lapis lazuli on the Ring of Thoth. Wispy white clouds slowly floated by, almost disappearing as a bird burst through them and flew off towards the horizon.

Cass blinked. The scene reminded her so much of her dream that she wasn't quite sure she was awake.

"Are we where I think we are?" asked Yo-Yoji.

"Well, we've been in this crate long enough," said Cass. "I mean, how long does it take to fly to Egypt?"

"I don't know; there's something very weird about this," said Max-Ernest. "This seems like a pretty big temple for a little cat mummy. You would think they'd just put him in a museum somewhere. Even in Egypt."

"Maybe this is a tourist site, and there's, like, one of those little museums connected to the ruins – and they're just storing the crate here until they unload it?" suggested Yo-Yoji.

"Maybe," said Max-Ernest. "Something about this doesn't make sense, though."

"C'mon, let's get out before somebody sees us," said Cass.

Still staring at their new surroundings, the three tired stowaways stepped out of the crate onto the stone floor of the temple and stretched their wobbly legs.

Before going any further, Yo-Yoji reached back into the crate and carefully removed his sunglasses from the face of the cat mummy. "Bye, little guy – it's been real."

He closed the door with more force than he meant to, and the bang echoed in the temple. They froze for a moment, waiting for the sound of Egyptian soldiers, but nobody came running. They still appeared to be alone.

Max-Ernest looked out at the vast desert vista. Snaking through the sand was a twisting line of green, and peeking through the vegetation was a sparkling river. "Is that…the Nile?" he asked.

"Let's go see," said Yo-Yoji, heading down the

temple steps. "Maybe we can catch a boat out of here."

"If we're where we think we are, it would take us a seriously long time to get home by boat," said Max-Ernest. "First, we'd have to travel up the Nile, then across the Mediterranean Sea—"

"You have a better idea?" asked Yo-Yoji.

Cass, overwhelmed by a sense of déjà vu, stopped halfway down the temple steps. "Isn't that the same bird we saw a moment ago?" she asked, scratching her head.

"What do you mean? How can you tell from here?" asked Max-Ernest.

"I can't – never mind."

Cass's sense of dreamlike unreality intensified as they stepped onto the sand. Each grain glittered in the sun like a tiny pebble of gold. She grabbed a fistful and let it fall from her hand like sand in an hourglass – it was her dream again.

"Watch out!" cried Yo-Yoji.

A large scorpion was scurrying across the sand towards them. They jumped back onto the temple steps. But it veered away before reaching them.

"Wow, that thing is huge – it's like a dog!" said Yo-Yoji, watching it go. "And so shiny. It almost looks like it's made of metal."

Tentatively, they stepped back into the sand.

The river had looked to be at least half a kilometre away, but it was much closer than that – perhaps ten metres. Indeed, as they walked towards it, they thought their eyes were playing tricks on them. Palm trees that from a distance had appeared to be six metres high now seemed hardly taller than they were.

When they were only a little way from the river, they looked down into the rushes.

"No boats," said Max-Ernest. "Time to make a new plan."

"What's that?" asked Cass, cocking her head to one side.

"Waaaa!" The crying came from the river.

"Is that a baby?!" asked Max-Ernest, who knew the sound only too well.

Indeed, it was – a baby swaddled in linen and lying in a basket. It looked as if it had floated down the river and become lodged in the papyrus plants along the shore. Crying at the top of its little lungs, the baby waved its arms and legs in the air.

Cass eyed the baby with concern. "Did somebody just leave it there?"

"Is anybody else remembering a story about a baby in the Nile?" asked Yo-Yoji.

The others looked blank.

"Um, the baby Moses? Sent down the river to be saved from being killed by the pharaoh's soldiers? Raised by an Egyptian princess? Gets the Ten Commandments? Neither of you two smarties ever heard of the Bible?"

"Sure, I've heard of it," said Cass defensively.

"So what are you saying – we got transported back to biblical times, and that's him right there?" asked Max-Ernest.

"I'm not saying anything. This whole thing is crazy."

"I don't care who it is – we can't just leave him like that," said Cass, stricken. "We have to do something." She started running towards the river.

Max-Ernest shook his head. "Hold on. Something's not – it's not real."

"What do you mean?" said Cass, slowing.

"Babies don't move like that. Trust me, I've spent the last year watching every move a baby makes, and a baby that little doesn't have that much motor coordination. And even if he did, the movements wouldn't repeat over and over – there would have to be a little variety, and then he would get tired. How 'bout that? I mean, babies *are* human beings. Sort of."

"You're saying it's a fake baby?" asked Cass. "Like a mechanical doll?"

"Just like this plant," said Yo-Yoji as they reached the river. He waved a papyrus plant around. It was plastic.

"And the sky," said Max-Ernest, pointing to a spot in a cloud that hid a loudspeaker. The sky was a painted backdrop.

Everything around them was fake. It was as if they were walking on a giant stage set. Only the water was real. And when they looked more closely at the river, they could see that the bottom was not sand but stucco.

"So where are we, then?" asked Cass.

"Just where we thought we were going," said Max-Ernest.

He nodded back at the temple. From this angle, they could see that one side of it was missing; it was a virtual stage set. Above the temple, neon letters blinked:

UNWRAPPED: REAL MUMMIES!

Clearly, this was the new home of the mummy exhibit.

In the middle of the sky was a sign:

CASINO

"Las Vegas? Sick." Yo-Yoji nodded.

Tired and hungry, they trudged through the sand towards the casino door, like refugees wandering the desert.

Given their exhausted state, it's no wonder they didn't notice the rustling in the artificial grass. Had their invisible stalker decided to pounce, he would have had the advantage of surprise. He decided to let them pass.

Here it would be too easy, he thought. This was Vegas. He wanted to gamble.

CHAPTER TWENTY-SIX

Eye in the Sky

It was like walking from day into night without ever going outside.

In contrast to the surreal quiet of the artificial desert, their current surroundings were a noisy blur of ringing bells, spinning wheels and flashing lights – and gleaming gold statues of Egyptian gods. This was the Cairo Hotel Casino.

"Whoa, this place is ridiculous," said Yo-Yoji.

"It's pretty big," concurred Max-Ernest.

"Yeah, and its carbon footprint is even bigger," said Cass. "Can you imagine how much energy is used in this one room? It's disgusting."

"Ever heard of fun?" asked Yo-Yoji.

Cass's eyes narrowed. "It's possible to have fun without wasting energy."

Max-Ernest couldn't help himself: "Well, technically, it's not possible to do anything without using energy, and I'm sure a certain amount is always—"

"Max-Ernest! Aargh!" groaned Cass. "Which way is out?"

"Yeah, let's motor," said Yo-Yoji. "Where's the bathroom? Does anyone else have to take a leak?"

They glanced around. The casino seemed to go on for ever in every direction. There were no visible exits – or even any visible walls. Instead, wherever they looked, there was another way to gamble.

WIN A PYRAMID OF GOLD

WIN WIN WIN

VALLEY OF THE KINGS BLACKJACK

CAIRO BINGO

NO-LIMIT POKER

TREASURE OF THE PHARAOH'S TOMB

KING TUT KENO

RAMSES ROULETTE

"We have to get home," said Cass, growing anxious.

So far, she reflected, their mission had been the Worst. Fail. Ever. Not only had they failed to find the mummy's finger, they'd been trapped inside a crate overnight and shipped far from home. They were suspected of stealing a mummy, and now the mummy's finger. They almost certainly weren't going to graduate, and they very well might wind up in jail. Meanwhile,

Lord Pharaoh, wherever he was, had nabbed the finger and was well on his way to resurrecting the mummy and learning the Secret. Only one thing stood in his way: the fact that Cass had the Ring of Thoth. She felt around her neck for the ring. It was still there. But at this rate, she would lose it soon enough.

Cass thought of Pietro's face when he'd learned that Dr. L had betrayed him again. Her heart sank. How much more disappointed would he be when he learned that Cass, his precious Secret Keeper, had lost the Secret for ever to the Midnight Sun?

"Why don't we try that way?" said Yo-Yoji, picking a direction at random. The others followed.

Almost as miserable as Cass, Max-Ernest looked down as they started walking. Beneath their feet was a seemingly endless blue and gold carpet with a pattern of scarabs and ankhs and other Egyptian symbols and hieroglyphs. Max-Ernest tried to make sense of what he was looking at, but it was soon clear to him that whoever had designed the carpet hadn't known what the symbols meant.

"They're oxymorons," he muttered.

"Who are?" asked Yo-Yoji.

"Nobody. The things on the floor. They all contradict each other."

"Shh," said Cass. "Let's try not to attract any

attention." She pointed to a sign: NO UNACCOMPANIED MINORS.

Yo-Yoji laughed. "Cheer up. This place is so loud you'd have to run screaming naked to attract attention. Nah, that wouldn't even do it. See."

He nodded to a long green craps table where a man was rolling dice while onlookers screamed in excitement and a nearly naked waitress served drinks.

Above the table, a sign blinked:

THE LUCKY MUMMY CRAPS
THROW YOUR BONES!

"Actually, all you really have to do to get attention is cheat," said Max-Ernest. "See that glass ball?"

He pointed to a small upside-down dome of glass in the ceiling. "People look through it, watching for cheaters and criminals and stuff. It's called the 'eye in the sky' – which is pretty funny because one of the symbols on the carpet is the eye of Horus, and Horus is the god of the sky. So it's like two sky-eyes staring at each other. How 'bout that?"

Yo-Yoji looked at him like he was crazy. "How do you know?"

"About Horus?"

"That thing in the ceiling."

"I read about it. A lot of magicians and comedians work in casinos, so I know a lot about them," said Max-Ernest. "Notice how there are no clocks or windows?"

"I know – it's so weird," said Cass. "You can't tell what time it is."

Max-Ernest nodded. "That's on purpose. So you keep gambling for ever. Think about it – it's the morning, right? All these people have probably been gambling all night."

"So if I put a quarter into this thing, I won't be able to stop until I spend all my money?" asked Yo-Yoji, approaching the nearest slot machine. It was decorated with an image of gold coins and a pair of hissing cobras. The words BRAVE THE CURSE – PLAY TO WIN THE PHARAOH'S GOLD flashed on and off.

"That's the idea."

"Okay, let's see," said Yo-Yoji.

"You can't. It's against the law!" said Max-Ernest, alarmed.

"I'll bet kids younger than me do this all the time," Yo-Yoji scoffed.

"Uh-huh. And they probably have people watching just for that reason."

"Max-Ernest is right," said Cass. "It's not a good time—"

Too late. Yo-Yoji had already dropped a quarter into the slot machine. "C'mon, let's live a little," he said, pulling the lever.

As soon as the wheels of the slot machine started to spin, a man in a dark suit with a walkie-talkie on his hip walked up to them.

"Hi, kids. Your parents around?"

"Uh, just outside," replied Yo-Yoji.

"Well, I suggest you go join them. If you're looking for games, try the Adventure Zone."

"That sounds great!" said Cass, with an *I-told-you-so* glare at Yo-Yoji. "But first – I know this is going to sound weird – how do we get out?"

"Just follow the Nile."

The security man pointed across the casino.

What had looked from far away like more sparkling slot machines was, in fact, the continuation of the faux river Nile reflecting the lights above. The river led them almost magically to the bathrooms and then to the main lobby of the hotel, where it momentarily vanished underground only to reappear outside the hotel's front doors.

Once outside, they could see that the Cairo Hotel had been built in the shape of a pyramid – "the biggest pyramid in the world", according to the hotel's promotional brochures. Of course, unlike an Egyptian pyramid, the hotel had sides made of glass. The glass was tinted gold, and when the sun hit the hotel – as it was hitting the hotel now – the building lit up like a volcano.

The pyramid sat back from the street, behind a vast plaza, and was surrounded by the river Nile like a castle surrounded by a moat. On either side of the plaza sat two stone sphinxes about the size of pickup trucks. In the centre of the plaza, the river ended in a large man-made lake that was dotted with lily pads, and in the centre of the lake was a tall glass obelisk that changed colours every few seconds. (For those who remember, it looked not unlike the ancient multicoloured flame that burned on top of the pyramid at the Midnight Sun Spa, but I would imagine that the obelisk was lit by ordinary coloured lights and controlled by a timer.) Around the obelisk, tall jets of water spouted and "danced" in time to music.

"It's like one huge environmental crime scene," Cass exclaimed. "Look at all that water! We're in the middle of the desert! How can these people live with themselves?"

She nodded to the throngs of tourists walking in and out of the hotel; she seemed to hold each of them personally responsible for turning a desert ecosystem into a glittering bastion of conspicuous consumption.

Giant gold-plated doors, each decorated with a giant eye of Horus, flanked the smaller, revolving glass doors that led into the hotel and casino. Guarding the doors were a half-dozen men in white cotton skirts and Egyptian headdresses. Their skin covered with chalk, they were so-called living statues, and they didn't blink when tourists snapped photos or kids taunted them.

"You think they would move if I yelled 'fire'?" asked Yo-Yoji.

"The question is, would *you* move?" said Cass. "Come on. We need to get home."

"Um, point made, but, uh, how?" asked Max-Ernest.

"How what?" asked Cass impatiently.

"How are we going to get home? You know, like planes, trains, automobiles?"

"Oh, that kind of *how*," said Cass. In her rush to get out of the hotel, she hadn't got that far in her thinking.

"We can't exactly expect to find another crate lying around," Max-Ernest pointed out.

"Hey, look who followed us to Las Vegas –" Yo-Yoji nodded discreetly towards the street, where the three

Priests of Amun they had seen by the Natural History Museum were now standing in their robes and turbans, holding their protest signs. One of them had a drum of some sort and was hitting it slowly and rhythmically; it sounded ominous.

Cass squinted. "Are they looking at us?"

Max-Ernest reacted with alarm. "You think they want to take revenge on us for breaking the mummy's finger? Maybe they think we have the mummy!"

Yo-Yoji laughed. "Now you're really losing it."

"Seems like if they were going to attack us, they already would have," said Cass.

"Unless they're waiting until there are less people around," said Max-Ernest. (To be grammatically correct, he should have said *fewer* people, but I'm afraid he was a bit nervous.) "Then they're going to drag us out into the scorching sun of the Nevada desert, perform some kind of ancient Egyptian curse ritual, and leave us to die of dehydration while scorpions sting us until we hallucinate about being eaten alive by an army of red ants crawling in and out of our eyeballs. How 'bout that?"

"Sick, man," said Yo-Yoji as if he were watching the scene in his head. "Think maybe the hunger's getting to you?"

"They didn't come here for us," said Cass, looking

up at a point between Max-Ernest and Yo-Yoji. "Or not *only* for us."

Yo-Yoji and Max-Ernest turned around, following her gaze. High above them, two construction workers were unveiling a huge pyramid-shaped billboard decorated with what looked like shimmering gold sequins:

THE CAIRO HOTEL
Presents

LORD PHARAOH
THE INVISIBLE MAGICIAN
LAS VEGAS'S LATEST ENTERTAINMENT SENSATION
IN
THE GOLDEN DAWN: THE MUMMY RISES
An Evening of Magic, Alchemy and Illusion

★ ★ ★ SPECIAL GUESTS THE SKELTON SISTERS ★ ★ ★

"Lord Pharaoh, *here*?" Max-Ernest took a step backwards.

"Lord Pharaoh, an *entertainment sensation*?" said Cass.

Yo-Yoji shook his head. "Not really keeping it on the low-profile tip, is he, Lord P?"

The three of them looked up again at the immense sign, larger than a small car, or even a big one – as, in fact, most things in Vegas seemed to be.

"What does he have to lose? Nobody can see him anyway. Which makes it pretty easy to do magic, by the way," said Max-Ernest bitterly. (He had been practising magic tricks for a few years now and was frustrated with his lack of progress.) "Anybody can disappear when they're invisible – that's cheating."

"Wait – *The Mummy Rises*?" Yo-Yoji looked up at the billboard again. "How can he do that without the ring?"

"He can't," said Cass simply. It was all becoming clear to her. "He's waiting for us to bring it to him."

Max-Ernest was confused. "Bring it to him? Where? When?"

"At the show."

"Why would we do that?!"

"Think about it. This is our chance. All we have to do is put the ring on the mummy's finger before Lord Pharaoh does, and we'll learn the Secret – well, I'll learn the Secret." She felt an electric tingle in her ears. The idea that the Secret was so close to her now – in this same city, on this same block, in this same hotel, even – was almost intoxicating. "Lord Pharaoh knows we have no choice."

Max-Ernest shook his head. "I knew it was too easy, the crate waiting open for us like that. Lord Pharaoh's been playing games with us the whole way. For all we know, he had them put that big billboard up just so we would see it!" Max-Ernest could feel himself starting to panic. "And now you want to deliver the ring to him on a platter?"

"Well, maybe he shouldn't be so sure of himself," said Cass defensively.

"But how're we supposed to get the finger from him in front of the whole audience? How do we bring the mummy to life before he does? How…how… anything?" Max-Ernest stammered in frustration.

"I don't know," said Cass. "We go to the show and we work it out when we get there. Just like we always do."

"See?" Yo-Yoji grinned. "It's all good."

"You understand we could be killed," said Max-Ernest. "Or worse."

Cass nodded. "I doubt he would kill us in front of all those people, but, yeah, it's a possibility."

"Come on, dude," said Yo-Yoji to Max-Ernest. "What do you want us to do – go home empty-handed? Then we're as good as dead anyway."

Max-Ernest shrugged. "We'll need tickets."

He knew when he was beaten. It happened quite often.

Pawns

Three coins. That was all the money they had left after purchasing one small soda for the three of them to share. To make matters worse, they were ancient coins, no longer legal tender anywhere in the world, let alone in Las Vegas.

On the bright side, the coins were gold. And worth a fortune.

How to turn them into cash? There was the rub.

"A pawnshop!"

It came to Max-Ernest in a flash. He'd never been to one. He wasn't sure he'd ever seen one. But he'd read about them in detective novels.

"You mean like in the movies, where a criminal sells off the stolen goods and then the police come looking for him at the shop that bought them?" asked Yo-Yoji.

"Right. It's called fencing," said Max-Ernest knowledgeably. "Only this time, *we*'re the criminals."

"Great idea," said Cass. "I've been in lots of pawnshops."

Her friends looked at her in surprise.

"My grandfathers had an antiques store, remember?" Cass stepped up the pace. "I bet Vegas has a bunch of pawnshops. All these people going broke..." She gestured disdainfully to the crowds of tourists and gamblers around them.

They were walking down the famous Las Vegas Strip, which was a bit like walking through an atlas come to life, with cartoon versions of Paris, Venice and New York right next to one another. Not to mention hotel roller coasters. White tigers. Wave machines. A life-size pirate's galleon. And all-you-can-eat prime rib for less than five dollars. All lit up by enough light bulbs to service all seven continents.

"Do you think we should go in the direction of the Eiffel Tower or the Statue of Liberty?" asked Max-Ernest.

"I think we should get off this street," said Cass.

When you're walking down the Strip, it's easy to think that Las Vegas is all flashy casinos, fancy hotels and oversized carnival rides. But only a short distance away, it's possible to find a very different sort of place.

On the block where they now found themselves, drunks were lying on the sidewalk, and uncollected garbage spilled out of cans. The buildings looked old and uncared for.

"Are we sure this is the best place to look?" Max-Ernest, by the sound of it, was far from sure.

"I've spent half my life going into pawnshops with my grandfathers – this is exactly the right kind of place," insisted Cass. Still, even she seemed a little nervous as she looked down the block.

Suddenly, she smiled and shook her head. "Look who's here!" She pointed to a man leaning against a store window several metres ahead of them. He looked like a bum – or a hobo – and he was wearing a familiar stained fisherman's hat with an old pigeon feather stuck in it.

"Owen! When did you get here?" Cass stepped up to the hobo, grinning wide. This time – finally – she had recognized him before he revealed himself. "You can stand up now and stop pretending. We found you."

The hobo looked at her. "My name is Mark, not that it's any of your business."

The kids looked more closely. There was no resemblance to Owen.

Cass's ears reddened in embarrassment. "Oh. Sorry. I thought I recognized your hat."

"This hat is mine. I stole it fair and square. You go steal your own!"

Cass nodded and hurried along. She was surprised at how disappointed she was. It had been comforting to think that Owen had come to Las Vegas in disguise to look after them, as he had so many times before.

Alas, they had nobody but themselves.

⋆ ⋆ ⋆

The first three pawnshops they tried were a bust, which is a colloquial way of saying that the pawnshop owners refused to give Cass money for her coins. The first two assumed the coins were fake, the third that they were stolen. Nobody believed that Cass had inherited them.

Luckily, there are more pawnshops in Las Vegas than there are gas stations – and luckily, too, there are much stranger things in Las Vegas than three children trying to sell a rare gold coin.

Not the third time but the fourth was the charm.

The Poor Man's Rich-in-Love Wedding Chapel and Pawnshop was a two-for-one business topped by an old neon sign. Every time the neon blinked, a heart would light up and a 1950s-style jitterbugging couple would kiss beneath it. The glass storefront was covered with so many plaques and posters that you couldn't see inside.

It's no gamble when you bet on love!

Something borrowed, something blue – everything you need for your wedding is here

Get married in minutes or your money back! No waiting ever!

TURN YOUR WEDDING PRESENTS INTO $ $ CASH $ $ AS SOON AS YOU GET THEM

Trade your watch for a wedding ring. Time flies when you're married!

FREE DIVORCE COUPON WITH EVERY MARRIAGE CERTIFICATE

A loud buzzer sounded when they walked into the pawnshop. The store was crowded with everything from rifles to saxophones to an old jukebox playing a song that seemed to be about old jukeboxes. Through an open door, they could see the back room: a makeshift wedding chapel decorated with plastic flowers and a pair of fake lovebirds in a dusty cage.

A sweaty man in a purple robe and a black square hat walked out and gave the three kids a cursory glance. A name tag on his chest read: PABLO, THE PAWNBROKER-PRIEST.

"A little young to be getting married, aren't we?

Well, I ain't prejudiced. Long as you got a note from your parents." He winked. "Now, which one of you boys is the lucky guy?"

"Neither!" said Max-Ernest quickly, his face turning red.

"That's not why we're here," said Yo-Yoji, whose face was turning a matching colour.

"Yeah, as if I would ever marry either one of them," said Cass with as much sarcasm as she could muster. She wouldn't have admitted it, but she was just the littlest bit hurt by the alacrity with which her friends denied that they were marrying her.

Max-Ernest studied the pawnbroker-priest. "Hey, isn't that a graduation robe? And that hat, too?" Their class had just ordered their graduation outfits, so he was well aware of what they looked like.

"So? The last priest who came in here – he had a winning streak and bought back his whole outfit. This is the only robe I got. Now what can I do you for?"

Cass reached into her backpack, pulling out her three gold coins.

The pawnbroker-priest laughed when he saw the coins. "Where'd you get these? From some pirate show down the Strip?" He screwed up his face, growling like a pirate. "Arrgh, matey."

"It's real gold, I swear," said Cass.

"Is that right? May I...?" He took the coins from her and felt their weight. "They *feel* real, I'll give you that." He looked at them under a small magnifying glass. "Very high-quality workmanship – you don't see counterfeit coins as good as these very often."

The pawnbroker-priest took a porcelain tile from his shelf. "Not much of a touchstone, but it usually works." He rubbed the coin on the tile to see what kind of mark it made.* "Huh," he said, non-committally.

Then he tried to scratch the window with the coin; there was no scratch. "Huh," he said again.

"Is that good? Or is it supposed to scratch?" asked Max-Ernest.

He didn't answer. But the kids could tell he was impressed.

Finally, he reached under the counter and pulled a magnet off a small refrigerator. When he held the magnet over the coin, the coin didn't move.

---

*A TOUCHSTONE IS A SMALL TABLET OF DARK STONE, SUCH AS FIELDSTONE OR SLATE, USED FOR ASSAYING (I.E., JUDGING THE COMPOSITION OF) PRECIOUS METALS. DRAWING A LINE OF GOLD ON A TOUCHSTONE LEAVES A VISIBLE TRACE, AND BECAUSE DIFFERENT GOLD ALLOYS HAVE DIFFERENT COLOURS, THIS LINE REVEALS HOW PURE THE PIECE OF GOLD IS. IN EVERYDAY SPEECH, A TOUCHSTONE MAY REFER TO ANYTHING BY WHICH OTHER THINGS OF ITS KIND ARE MEASURED. FOR EXAMPLE, *WHEN IT COMES TO LITERARY GENIUS, THE BOOKS OF PSEUDONYMOUS BOSCH PROVIDE A TOUCHSTONE.*

"Huh," he said once more.

He bent over the counter and studied Cass and her friends as closely as he had the coins. Finally, he placed the coins carefully on a black square of cloth on the counter and offered his verdict:

"All right, so maybe the coins are gold."

The three tried not to react, but the pawnbroker-priest bristled at their slightest stir – attuned, as he was, to the smallest detail of any transaction.

"Maybe. But that doesn't mean they're really five hundred years old. And if they are, they're obviously not yours. They've got to be either hot or fake, or both, but I like you guys, so I'll take them. Also, three gold coins – it's good luck for a pawnbroker."

He pointed to the design on his store window: it was the same as the design they'd seen on the other stores. What they'd thought were three gold berries hanging from branches were actually three gold coins, the ancient symbol of the pawnshop.

"I've only got enough cash for one coin, but I can give you cheques for the others?"

They shook their heads. Cheques wouldn't do them any good.

After a good ten minutes of haggling, during which the kids tried unsuccessfully to get him to give them more money, the pawnbroker-priest took one coin and gave them an amount approximately equal to one-tenth of its true value. Which, as it turned out, was quite a lot.

In cash.

"You want a bag for that?" the man asked as Cass tried unsuccessfully to stuff all the money into her backpack.

"No, it's fine," she said as hundred-dollar bills floated down to the ground, crumpling and ripping beneath her feet. The man just shook his head and, reaching behind the counter, grabbed a small ziplock bag. Snack-size.

Cass looked from the bag to the pile of bills.

The man sighed and shook his head again – painful as it was to part with all that nice green cash – and pulled out a larger bag. The litre size.

Max-Ernest gestured, with his hands full of green.

"All right, all right." The pawnbroker-priest pulled out a bag large enough to hold a small child. "On the house. Now get out of here before I change my mind and call the cops. Or your parents!"

Nile Nails

The box office for the Pyramid Theatre, where Lord Pharaoh would be performing that night, was located in its own kiosk between the Adventure Zone, the indoor kids' theme park that our underage heroes had been hearing so much about, and the Sphinx Shops, the Cairo Hotel's "famed boutique district", where you could find everything from luggage (Luxor Luggage) to a nail salon (Nile Nails) to a pet salon (King Muttenkhamen's Royal Beauty Parlour).

As Cass led her friends to the ticket line for Lord Pharaoh's show, they eyed the entrance to the Adventure Zone with a combination of envy and scorn.

PARENTS AWAY! KIDS HOORAY!
Bungee jump into the pharoah's tomb!
Climb the rock wall with live monkeys!
SING! DANCE! MAKE YOUR OWN RAP VIDEO!
The longest zip line in Las Vegas!
No one over 18 allowed!

"I'll bet a lot of parents throw their kids into the Adventure Zone so they can keep gambling," said Cass disdainfully.

Yo-Yoji laughed. "Oh, so now you think parents shouldn't let their kids be by themselves? You disapprove or something?"

"I think parents should be parents."

"What about your mom?" Max-Ernest asked. "Do you think she shouldn't give you so much freedom?"

"That's different."

"How?"

"It just is. Do I have to explain everything?"

Yo-Yoji and Max-Ernest looked at each other and shook their heads.

Cass dropped the heavy backpack to the mosaic floor in front of the box-office window.

"Three tickets, please." She swallowed, looking at the poster behind the cashier's head. The words one night only seemed to jump out at her.

"Balcony, orchestra, or premier?" the cashier said without looking up.

"I don't know. What's premier?"

"Front-row seats with a backstage pass." The cashier – a woman whose nails were longer than her nose – peered over the edge of the counter. "Balcony will be cheapest, sweetheart. You probably want those."

Cass pulled a fistful of one-hundred-dollar bills out of her backpack. "I'll take three premiers."

The cashier raised an eyebrow. "You kids weren't playing the slots, I hope?"

Cass shook her head.

"Daddy's on a winning streak?"

"Something like that."

The cashier nodded wisely. "Well, spend it while you can, doll – that's my advice. Trust me, he'll want it all back by the end of the night."

"Okay, there are two hours left before the show," said Yo-Yoji as they walked away with their tickets. "We could spend that time carefully planning how to deal with Lord Pharaoh, knowing that it probably won't make any difference and we're going to be killed anyway. Or we could spend our last two hours on earth having fun." He nodded in the direction of the Adventure Zone. "What do you say?"

"I don't know – planning can be fun," said Max-Ernest.

Yo-Yoji eyed him askance. "That was a joke, right?"

Cass looked at the signs covering the Adventure Zone, battling her conscience. "Well," she said finally, "maybe it wouldn't hurt to try the zip line. I mean, it could be good training... for, you know, if we have to, like, swing from the pulleys and stuff on the stage tonight."

"Exactly what I was thinking," said Yo-Yoji

emphatically. "What we need right now is a serious training session."

But first things first. As soon as they walked into the Adventure Zone, the still-starving kids treated themselves to hot-fudge sundaes at Osiris's Ice Cream Oasis. The sundaes were huge – like everything in Las Vegas – and built to their custom specifications. Cass ordered the Ra, which came with ribbons of caramel sauce and peanut butter chips. Yo-Yoji's Oasis Special was served inside a pineapple and was surrounded by tropical fruit. Max-Ernest, of course, ordered the Chocolate Pyramid: chocolate ice cream, chocolate fudge and chocolate chips. All the sundaes came with mountains of whipped cream, toasted almond slivers, and clown-nose-red maraschino cherries on top. Max-Ernest hesitated about the whipped cream, fearing it would dilute the strength of the chocolate, but ultimately he gave in, deciding that sometimes more is more. He was not disappointed.

Halfway through her sundae, Cass stopped with her spoon in mid-air, realizing how fast and greedily she'd been eating. Not only was it disgusting, she reprimanded herself, it was unhealthy. It was bad enough to consume so many carbohydrates on an empty stomach – her blood-sugar level was going to spike – but if she kept eating so fast, she was going to make herself sick, and she needed to be in top form for the battle ahead.

She looked up at her friends, thinking she should caution them to slow down, and saw a frightful sight: Yo-Yoji and Max-Ernest, crazed looks in their eyes, faces smeared with whipped cream and chocolate, were holding two spoons each. They were in such a frenzy, *both* of them were eating with *both* hands, double-fisting their sundaes.

"I . . . think . . . maybe . . . I . . . might . . . just . . . possibly . . . get . . . another . . . one," said Max-Ernest, who literally was licking his bowl clean to get the last bits of fudge.

Shaking her head, Cass ripped the spoons out of her friends' hands. It was time for their training session.

It's amazing how many activities you can fit into a single hour if you have enough motivation and enough cash. After hurtling themselves, screaming, across the "longest zip line in Las Vegas", the kids climbed thirty metres and bungee jumped into a "pharaoh's tomb". (Well, Cass and Yo-Yoji jumped. Max-Ernest, it would be more accurate to say, was pushed.) They floated in zero gravity (actually, a wind tunnel) until they were ready to regurgitate their sundaes; they rode mechanical camels until they were thrown off into artificial sand dunes; and they played skee-ball until, well, they got a little bored. Yo-Yoji even managed to persuade his friends to try their luck at the "Dance like an Egyptian" hip-hop dance steps arcade game. (They made him promise not to tell Amber.) But Cass drew the line at making her own rap video. Not only did she not believe in such egregious acts of digital self-aggrandizement, but there was something else she wanted to do. She told them she would meet them outside the Adventure Zone thirty minutes later.

"Knock yourselves out," she said, handing Yo-Yoji a one-hundred-dollar bill.

She could hear her friends practising as she walked away:

"Don't be a fool, yo, Lord Pharaoh will put you in the ground for life. / That's cool, yo, if I go home, my parents will ground me for life."

A moment later, Cass looked over her shoulder to make sure Yo-Yoji and Max-Ernest weren't watching as she walked into Nile Nails. It was silly, maybe, but she couldn't help being embarrassed about what she was doing. No doubt they would make fun of her later, but if they made fun of her now, she feared she wouldn't have the nerve to go through with it.

She'd never been to a nail salon before.

Her mother, who complained frequently about the state of Cass's fingernails, had repeatedly tried to get Cass to have a manicure, but Cass struck back by barraging her mother with statistics about the various types of infections you could pick up in nail salons. (Fungal infections, yeast infections, staph infections – the list was long and hideous.) She was so persuasive that her mother had given up on going to nail salons herself, and now her mother's fingernails were almost as bad as hers.

"Hi, I'm Felicia," said a smiling woman in a smock. She was dressed like a dental technician, save for her long, gold, rhinestone-encrusted fingernails and matching gold- and rhinestone-beaded cornrows.

"Are you ready to be pampered like a queen? We're running a special on a full mani-pedi – oh, dear," she said, getting a look at Cass's fingernails for the first time. "It's sort of a code-red situation, isn't it? Your cuticles have grown all the way over your nails. Please don't tell me your toenails are just as bad."

"Well, I haven't been chewing on them, if that's what you mean," said Cass, her ears flaming red.

Cass tried to refuse the pedicure outright; she was afraid that if she took her shoes off, she wouldn't be able to run out of the room on a moment's notice. In the end, however, she consented to the super-deluxe treatment – the Nefertiti Special – which included a hand-and-foot massage and soak, cuticle "relief" (a euphemism, it turned out, for painful cuticle butchery), fingernail *and* toenail trim and buff, three coats of polish, and a choice of "authentic" Egyptian nail decals.

She fought Felicia the whole way, insisting that all instruments that touched her fingers or feet be not only sterilized but brand-new. Even when Felicia had to switch out the standard emery board for industrial sandpaper to sand down the calluses on her heels, Cass insisted on only the freshest sandpaper imaginable. (The tall pile of dead grey skin that formed a pyramid of its own under each of her heels was a testament to how hard both Felicia and the sandpaper were working.) When it came time to choose a nail polish, Cass asked for clear – but when urged repeatedly to try a colour, she relented and agreed to Cleopatra blue, which reminded her of the lapis lazuli on the Ring of Thoth.

She was drowsily admiring her new nails – the blue gave them a space-age, almost alien quality that she didn't entirely dislike, as well as complementing nicely the baby pink of her newly sanded skin – when Felicia returned with a spiral notebook.

"And now's when we turn you into an Egyptian princess!" She opened the notebook to a page of sparkling peel-off Egyptian symbols. "Do you want to choose, honey?"

"No, just surprise me."

The first three decals were predictable: a scarab, an ankh, and an eye of Horus. The fourth, however, made Cass sit up, suddenly wide awake.

"What's that?" she asked as Felicia carefully applied the decal to Cass's pinkie nail.

"Just another sticker, honey."

"No, I mean, it's a hieroglyph, right? Does it mean something?"

Made up of three wavy lines, one on top of the other, the hieroglyph was very simple, and Cass had seen it many times in her hunt for the hieroglyphs of the Secret. But seeing it now curving around her nail made her realize she'd seen it before – on papyrus. It was the fourth hieroglyph of the Secret. She was certain. It had almost been staring her in the face all along. Since so much of the original hieroglyph had been smudged, she'd always assumed there was more to it – that the three lines were part of a grid making a building or something of that nature.

"That hieroglyph?" Felicia laughed. "Yes, I know it. That one's right on the window."

In fact, it was on the window of the very salon Cass was sitting in.

"This is Nile Nails, right? That's the sign for the Nile, but a customer told me it usually just means *river* or *water*. Hey, you're not a water sign, are you? You seem more like an Aries. But you could be a Cancer, maybe..."

River. Water. Nile.

Because what ibis/Thoth river/water/Nile walk/run/ cross...

That was the Secret – as far as she'd been able to make out.

What did it mean? That the Secret was something about Thoth walking next to a river? Or over a river? Maybe *through* a river? Could it be something like the parting of the Red Sea?[*]

And what was the *what*? Was the *what* the thing that allowed Thoth to walk the river? Was the *what* the secret of the Secret? It was still so confusing.

She hoped the Ring of Thoth would reveal the answer. How? She had no idea.

"Cass! There you are! We've been looking all over."

---

[*]THE PARTING OF THE RED SEA, AS YOU MAY RECALL, IS PART OF THE STORY OF MOSES AND THE EXODUS FROM EGYPT. AS YO-YOJI HAD SURMISED, CASS HAD NEVER HAD MUCH OF A RELIGIOUS EDUCATION. NONETHELESS, IN THE COURSE OF HER STUDIES OF SUCH THINGS AS PLAGUES (MODERN AS WELL AS ANCIENT), DYING FROGS (A SURE SIGN OF ENVIRONMENTAL CATASTROPHE) AND RED SEAS (THE KIND CAUSED BY ALGAE), SHE'D COME ACROSS THE STORY OF THE EXODUS SEVERAL TIMES.

"We were worried, yo."

Max-Ernest and Yo-Yoji were walking towards her.

"What are you doing here?"

"What happened to your nails?"

"Hi," said Cass. She'd been so consumed with her thoughts about the Secret that she'd forgotten all about her friends. And about her fingernails. She wanted to hide them in her fist, but she was worried they were still wet. So instead she spread her fingers wide.

"Go ahead," she said. "Give me your best shot. Let me have it."

"No, no, they look...nice," said Yo-Yoji.

"Yeah...nice," said Max-Ernest.

"You bet they do!" said Felicia angrily. "Have some respect. This here is an Egyptian princess, and for the rest of the day you must address her as Your Royal Highness. Make that Your Royal *Hotness*!"

"Okay, for sure, will do," said Yo-Yoji. He looked at Cass, barely able to contain his laughter. "Is Your Royal Hotness ready to go?"

"Yeah, we're late, Your Royal Hotness." Max-Ernest doubled over. He couldn't help it.

Cass punched him, even though Felicia tried to hold her back. "Think of your nails!"

A Special Note to the Midnight Sun

YOU MISSED.

I'M STILL HERE.

NEXT TIME, TRY A LITTLE TARGET PRACTICE FIRST.

NOW
IF YOU'LL EXCUSE ME, I'M RIGHT
IN THE MIDDLE OF TELLING
A REALLY GOOD STORY.

The
Golden Finger

When they entered the theatre lobby, they found themselves surrounded by images of Lord Pharaoh – depicted as the shadowy outline of a man in a gold cape. Seemingly overnight, the "Invisible Magician", as he was called, had become an industry unto himself. Kiosks sold Lord Pharaoh T-shirts and posters. There were DVDs and calendars. There was even a magic set that came in a big gold box; Max-Ernest looked at it wistfully. Cass might have let him buy it, too, had the timing been better – and had Lord Pharaoh's name not been on it.

"Can you believe – all this stuff for that creep?" asked Cass. "He sure works fast."

"Actually, a calendar is pretty easy to make," said Yo-Yoji. "You could make most of this stuff in under an hour if you wanted."

"Sheesh! Listen to what they're saying," said Max-Ernest.

Everybody around them was talking about Lord Pharaoh:

"Supposedly, he's just a shimmering cloud of dust – you never see him!" "It's like he's really invisible..." "They say he's the greatest magician since Houdini..."

"That's an insult to Houdini," Max-Ernest muttered, offended.

Cass shushed him, and they filed into the theatre.

It was a vast, Vegas-size theatre, with a mezzanine and several balcony levels. As they found their seats near the stage in the orchestra section, the audience continued to buzz with anticipation:

"I heard he's a real alchemist. He can actually turn lead into gold!" *"Even other magicians don't know how he does it..."* *"Is it true he'll turn your watch into gold right in front of everybody?"*

Cass rolled her eyes. "What they don't know is they could be just as amazing as Lord Pharaoh – all they'd have to do is eat Señor Hugo's chocolate," she whispered, sitting down.

"I thought there wasn't any more chocolate left," Yo-Yoji said, sitting down next to her. "So they couldn't eat it, even if they knew about it."

"We don't know that," said Max-Ernest, sitting on the other side of Cass. "I keep thinking, for him to have got this far, he must have figured out how to make the chocolate himself."

"Anyway, that's not the point," said Cass. "The point is, he's a jerk, and all these people think he's a genius. He's like the Wizard of Oz – just a little old guy behind a velvet curtain."

"Actually, the Wizard of Oz was a time traveller, too, come to think of it," Max-Ernest mused. "Remember, he's that quack medicine salesman from Dorothy's own time who winds up in Oz, just like her? Well, I guess Kansas-to-Oz isn't time travel, technically. More like inter-dimensional travel. Or is it *intra*-dimensional? I always forget the difference..."

Yo-Yoji gave Max-Ernest one of his increasingly frequent *you-are-totally-insane* looks.

"Shh, they're starting," said Cass.

Their expressions grew serious as the lights dimmed. Jerk or genius or both, Lord Pharaoh had bested them in the past. They would need all their wits about them if they were going to get through the evening unscathed.

"Welcome to Golden Dawn," said a soothing voice over a loudspeaker. "No cameras and no recording devices, please. Anybody caught recording the show will be escorted out of the theatre immediately."

Cass nudged her friends: guards with headsets stood at all four corners of the room and by the exit doors.

She was relieved to see that the guards weren't wearing gloves, but it also made her nervous. Where was the Midnight Sun? Why hadn't *they* shown up anywhere?

★　★　★

The stage was dark.

An orchestra began to play, first softly, then more loudly, until it opened up into the big brassy beginning of the James Bond theme song "Goldfinger".

Two identical female voices began to sing in duet about "the man with the Midas touch, a spider's touch".*

Suddenly, spotlights created circles at opposite ends of the stage. In each circle stood a slim young woman with long blonde hair, wearing a clingy gold bodysuit. Or maybe I should say young-*seeming* woman. For these were the Skelton Sisters. Young by the standards of the Midnight Sun, they were at least forty years old by any reasonable estimation – and yet they still looked, talked, and behaved like teenagers.

"Which one is Romi, and which one is Montana?" Max-Ernest whispered. "I can't tell them apart."

"Don't know, don't care," said Cass. "Thought we'd never have to see them again."

---

*GOLDFINGER IS THE VILLAIN IN THE JAMES BOND MOVIE OF THE SAME NAME. OBSESSED WITH GOLD, HE KILLS A WOMAN BY PAINTING HER ENTIRE BODY WITH IT. MIDAS IS A FIGURE FROM GREEK MYTHOLOGY WHO LITERALLY HAD THE GOLDEN TOUCH: EVERYTHING HE TOUCHED TURNED TO GOLD, EVEN HIS FAMILY. AS FOR A SPIDER'S TOUCH, THAT'S SOMETHING I EXPERIENCE ALL TOO OFTEN IN MY CURRENT HIDEOUT. CURSE THESE CREATURES!

"Wishful thinking," said Yo-Yoji.

The sisters continued to sing about the sinister Mr. Goldfinger and his "web of sin", swaying in unison and wagging their fingers like Motown singers of old.

More stage lights came on, revealing several dozen scantily clad dancers, male and female, whose bare skin was covered with gold body paint. They flipped and spun and twirled in an acrobatic blur of golden limbs and torsos.

Then, as the song ended, the dancers receded into the background and Lord Pharaoh's voice echoed throughout the theatre. It seemed to come from everywhere and nowhere at once:

"Gold. The most malleable of metals, and the most precious. A symbol of power and perfection. Of royalty and immortality. It never tarnishes..."

A light – first dim, then brighter – shone on the centre of the stage, revealing a gleaming gold coffin. It bore no hieroglyphs or markings of any kind, but it had the unmistakable shape of an Egyptian sarcophagus.

"The ancient Egyptians adorned the dead with gold to pave their way to the afterlife," Lord Pharaoh continued. His voice was sonorous and authoritative, with just a trace of his sixteenth-century European roots. "The Spanish conquistadores sailed the globe, courting death and disaster, in their search for El Dorado, the mythical City of Gold. Today, gold is placed around the necks of Olympians and on the heads of kings. But it was the medieval alchemists who loved gold best. In their quest for the philosopher's stone, they strove to turn ordinary objects into gold and hence to achieve the greatness of Midas. Their dream is alive tonight!"

The lid of the gold sarcophagus rose slowly into the air and then stopped, seeming to hover about two metres above the base.

"Allow me to introduce myself..."

As the music reached a crescendo, the Skelton Sisters stepped forward. Simultaneously, each threw a handful of shimmering gold dust in the direction of the sarcophagus.

"I am Lord Pharaoh."

The crowd gasped.

The shadow of a man – literally the *outline* of a man, but *shadow* better describes the effect – had emerged in the shimmering dust and was now stepping out of the sarcophagus.

Cass grabbed Max-Ernest's hand. Yo-Yoji grabbed Cass's arm. Max-Ernest screwed shut his eyes.

They couldn't believe what they were seeing. Even

though they'd been looking for him – even though they'd hawked the coin and bought the tickets and waited to see him – it was almost too terrible to watch now that he was here.

"But I am not only Lord Pharaoh. I am all the pharaohs of the past... and future."

As he spoke, one of the Skelton Sisters held up a long cape of gold satin and draped it over his shimmering-dust shoulders. The cape was topped with a big gold collar and appeared to float in the air. Scarabs and eyes of Horus and other Egyptian symbols were embroidered into the fabric. The other Skelton Sister placed a crown on his shimmering head. (Max-Ernest recognized it as the double crown worn by pharaohs to symbolize the union of Upper and Lower Egypt.)

Meanwhile, the Skelton Sisters reprised the "Goldfinger" chorus.

As gold dust floated to the ground, Lord Pharaoh grew fainter and fainter, until he was nearly invisible underneath his cape. Just as he was about to disappear altogether, he held a single solid-gold finger aloft.

An image of the finger, magnified many times over, appeared on a silver screen behind him – so that people in the back rows could see it. Although it appeared to be made of gold, it was thin and bony and crooked. There was no mistaking whose finger it was.

"That's it – the mummy's finger!" Yo-Yoji whispered.

"He must have dipped it in gold or something," said Max-Ernest.

When the music died down, the Skelton Sisters removed Lord Pharaoh's cape and crown. All that was left for the audience to see was the mummy's golden finger, shown on the screen again, and the barest hint of gold dust.

"The gold finger that you see once graced the hand of the greatest doctor in ancient Egypt – a man who knew the most precious Secret in the universe," intoned the invisible Lord Pharaoh. "This man is now a mummy. Soon, through the power of gold, he will live again!"

The audience murmured in awe as images of ancient Egypt flickered behind him.

The Skelton Sisters rolled the golden sarcophagus to the centre of the stage. As ominous music played, it began to rise in the air. When it was a little way off the ground, it began tilting further and further forward, until it was floating upright.

"Behold – the mummy!"

As Lord Pharaoh spoke, the lid of the sarcophagus

floated away. A spotlight revealed the sarcophagus's occupant: the mummy.

"When I have brought him back to this world from the next, he will be my slave, and I will possess all his power."

Lord Pharaoh murmured a few words in ancient Egyptian, then translated: "O mighty Thoth, let this finger rejoin the hand of its master."

The finger glowed a fiery orange as he reattached it to the mummy's hand. From where our friends sat, it looked like pure magic, but of course it also was possible that he was using glue.

Behind Lord Pharaoh, hieroglyphs appeared on the screen. They looked as though they were being burned into a sheet of gold.

"I have only to place the golden Ring of Thoth onto the mummy's finger, and this once-great man will breathe once more."

"I don't get it," Max-Ernest said to Cass. "You still have the ring, don't you?"

She touched her neck. "Uh-huh."

"Not for long," said Yo-Yoji darkly. "Look who's coming—"

His friends turned just in time to see their old adversary Daisy hoisting Yo-Yoji out of his seat. "Hey, let go of me—!" cried Yo-Yoji.

"Gladly," said the massive Midnight Sun member. She tossed him into the aisle as if he weighed no more than a pillow.

"Aak!" He held his shoulder in pain.

The audience murmured nervously.

Lord Pharaoh guffawed loudly. "Ha! Do not be alarmed, Ladies and Gentlemen. All part of the show, of course... And now if my lovely assistant, Cassandra, will please bring me the ring—"

A spotlight fell on Cass where she was sitting. Suddenly, an entire roomful of eyes were on her. She shrank back in her seat.

Daisy reached for Cass. "You, come with me."

"No way! You can't take her," said Max-Ernest bravely.

"Do not worry; this is only a game," Lord Pharaoh reassured his audience. "Cassandra, she likes to play – what is the contemporary expression? – hard to get."

The audience laughed, like any good Vegas audience – probably because a track of pre-recorded laughter cued them in the background.

Cass, on the other hand, did not feel like laughing at all.

She looked over at Yo-Yoji for help, but he was now being held by two security guards. She looked in the other direction – there were guards waiting in the opposite aisle. There was no escape.

"Don't fight! Then they'll take you, too," she whispered to Max-Ernest.

He didn't fight, but they took him anyway.

The Ring
of Thoth

Their arms pinned behind their backs, Yo-Yoji and Max-Ernest watched in horror as Daisy escorted – or, more accurately, dragged – Cass down the aisle and into the orchestra pit.

As soon as Cass disappeared, they were dragged in the opposite direction – and out the exit. The guards pushed them roughly into the lobby. Then – wordlessly – the guards went back into the auditorium.

Yo-Yoji stared suspiciously at the doors closing behind the guards. "Why did they let us go?"

"Because Lord Pharaoh doesn't care about us – Cass has what he wants," said Max-Ernest. "But what are we going to do?"

"Well, we could always try these." Yo-Yoji gestured to the badges hanging from their necks: each one said BACKSTAGE PASS in big black letters.

The entrance to the backstage area might have been exclusive, but it was hardly hidden. On the contrary, it was advertised with a large illuminated sign.

BACKSTAGE AREA
PREMIER TICKET HOLDERS ONLY

Max-Ernest and Yo-Yoji were glad to see that the bouncer standing at the velvet rope was not wearing gloves. Appearing not to recognize the two of them, he checked their badges, then waved them in as if it were perfectly natural that they would want to take advantage of their backstage access.

They didn't have a plan yet, but at least they were getting back inside.

Daisy pushed Cass onto the stage, then receded into the wings.

Cass tried to take stock of her surroundings and create a mental map of all potential pitfalls and hazards, not to mention enemy combatants. But her attention was drawn inexorably to the centre of the stage, where the mummy was still floating upright in the open sarcophagus. Here, just a few metres away, was the thing she had so desperately been seeking, and she couldn't take her eyes off it.

The last time she'd seen Amun, the mummy's bandages were wound tightly around him. Now they were loose and frayed. His hands, previously bound to his waist, were hanging free at his sides. His parched face and gaping mouth, however, looked just as they had before – equal parts haunted and haunting. Hanging from a tree on Halloween, he would have scared the heck out of a trick-or-treater, it occurred to Cass. But the mummy wasn't a Halloween decoration, he was...

Well, what *was* this thing, this body, this corpse, this man, this...whatever it was? Skin and bones – was that all? *No, there are also teeth, and fingernails, and dried fleshy tissues*, she could hear Max-Ernest saying. But that wasn't the point. He never got the point.

"Look – it's back," hissed Romi (or was it Montana?), snapping Cass back to the present.

"Yeah, we just can't get rid of it," hissed Montana (or was it Romi?).

"*It*...is happy to leave anytime," said Cass sarcastically. Microphones hanging from the stage picked up her words, and they reverberated through the auditorium.

"No, please, stay," purred the invisible Lord Pharaoh.

"Where are you?" asked Cass, pulling her monocle out of her pocket.

"I'm right here," answered Lord Pharaoh before she could put the monocle to her eye.

She jumped. Lord Pharaoh was so close she could feel his breath.

"I'm glad you found your way here."

She looked at him through the monocle. He smiled

an awful smile, knowing she could see him now.

"For a second, I thought you might not be foolish enough to fall into my trap," he whispered. "But I see you took the bait."

"Oh, I wouldn't miss this show for the world!" said Cass loudly.

She had already decided there was nothing to be gained by fighting. It would only wear her out. Her sole strategy was to buy time. It wasn't much of a strategy, true, but in her experience, opportunities usually presented themselves if you waited long enough. Everybody's armour showed its chinks eventually.

She lowered her voice. "But as my friend Max-Ernest pointed out, it's pretty easy to do illusions when you're invisible."

"True enough." Lord Pharaoh snatched the monocle out of her hand, making himself invisible to Cass again. "Of course, this sort of magic is child's play for someone who is involved in the real Work."

"You mean alchemy, right?"

"Alchemy, that's right... Nonetheless, our audience is waiting." He raised his voice: "The ring, please."

"Um –"

Cass pretended to fumble for the ring like a best man at a wedding.

"Oops! I think I dropped it!"

Max-Ernest and Yo-Yoji raced down the hallway, past rooms full of props and costumes. Many of these items obviously had not been used in years and were displayed for tourists, but some of the rooms seemed to be bustling.

"Can I help you?" A uniformed attendant tried to stop them with a smile. "Would either of you like a drink?"

"No, thanks!" Yo-Yoji called out as they continued running.

"Wait, what's that?" asked Max-Ernest.

"What?" Yo-Yoji turned to see Max-Ernest standing frozen, his nose twitching.

"I smell...chocolate."

"So what? There's no time—"

"*Dark* chocolate..." said Max-Ernest, his eyes glazed.

"Yo, dude – you just had all that hot fudge fifteen minutes ago. How can you even—?"

"Wait, just a minute, I have to—"

Max-Ernest darted into the nearest door, the one with a star on it – and the freshly painted name LORD PHARAOH.

Yo-Yoji looked in after Max-Ernest. "There's nothing in here!"

That was an exaggeration. Lord Pharaoh's dressing room was large and luxurious, with a sitting area on one side; on the other side were a long counter and a mirror surrounded by vanity lights. A tall vase with an extravagant bouquet of flowers sat on an end table by a couch. (Had either Max-Ernest or Yo-Yoji bothered to look, they would have seen a card hanging from the flowers, signed *Bon chance, Antoinette*.) But it was true: the room looked remarkably empty.

"Dude, if you don't come out this second, I swear—"

Max-Ernest didn't appear to hear a word Yo-Yoji was saying. Like a hunting dog trying to catch a scent, he stood in the middle of the room with his nose in the air.

"Forget it. I'm just going to go rescue Cass by myself."

"No, no, wait," said Max-Ernest.

Following his nose, Max-Ernest walked slowly towards the end of the counter. He looked positively bewitched.

"Here," he said when he reached the back corner. He held up his hand, victorious.

"What? There's nothing in your hand."

"Feel," said Max-Ernest, walking out of the room. "It's chocolate. Guess Lord Pharaoh thought he didn't have to hide it 'cause it's invisible. How 'bout that?"

Yo-Yoji reached for Max-Ernest's hand. Sure enough, he felt a bar. Max-Ernest yanked it away.

"Not just any chocolate. I've only smelled this once before, but I'd recognize it anywhere," said Max-Ernest, holding the invisible chocolate to his nose and inhaling greedily. "It's Señor Hugo's chocolate. Time Travel Chocolate. I *knew* Lord Pharaoh had mastered the formula! It was the only way he could have got here..."

With a crazed look in his eye, he moved his hand towards his mouth.

"Don't!" Yo-Yoji grabbed Max-Ernest's wrist. "You can't. Plus, there's no time to lose—"

Max-Ernest shuddered, coming to his senses. "Sorry. You're right. I don't know what happened. That would have been a disaster."

"No sweat."

"But you just gave me an idea. There *is* time to lose. Lord Pharaoh's time. Five hundred years of it."

"Say what?"

"I'll explain on the way." Max-Ernest started running down the hallway again.

Yo-Yoji followed close behind, keeping an eye on his friend's hand. They had enough problems already, without Max-Ernest eating his way into another century.

As Cass pretended to look on the floor for the ring, she felt one hand grab her arm and another hand grab her necklace.

"Ow!" The chain bit into her neck. Cass could feel herself choking. She struggled, but it was no use.

"So sorry," said Lord Pharaoh, not letting go. He tugged harder and harder, until the chain broke.

Cass clutched her throat, gasping for air. "I knew I didn't like necklaces," she said under her breath.

"Thank you," said Lord Pharaoh. Holding the Ring of Thoth in his invisible fist, he let the chain drop to the floor. "Ladies and Gentlemen, can we have a hand for the young Cassandra."

The applause track resumed. The Skelton Sisters clapped stiffly, like hosts of a game show.

"You may take a seat now, Cassandra," said Lord Pharaoh. Two gold-painted musclemen came up behind her and gripped her from both sides.

"No, thanks, I think I'll stay," said Cass. She still didn't know how she was going to stop him, but she had to try.

"All the better! You shall see my victory up close," said Lord Pharaoh. "Men – the jars!"

At his command, two of the gold musclemen wheeled in front of her a large platform on which sat four gold jars, each just over a metre tall. Before Cass could protest, one of the men opened the lid of the first jar. The other man hoisted her in the air and dropped her in. They lowered the lid – which had a hole in the middle for her head – and closed it around her, locking the lid in place with clamps. Her head stuck out the top, and she wore a furious expression on her face.

"You recognize canopic jars, of course. For storing the organs of the dead. Later, I will perform for the audience a great trick – and spread your severed parts among the four jars. But for now, please enjoy the spectacle," said Lord Pharaoh gallantly.

"Thanks," said Cass through gritted teeth. She could hear Lord Pharaoh's footsteps as he walked over to the mummy.

He's wearing boots, she thought.

"And now the moment that everyone has been waiting for, but none more so than I."

A spotlight illuminated the Ring of Thoth as his invisible hand held it over the mummy. The ring appeared to hover in the air.

Again Lord Pharaoh spoke in ancient Egyptian, and

again he translated. "Mighty Thoth, for what – why – must you take the life of this man?"

Burning hieroglyphs appeared behind Lord Pharaoh. Two of them Cass recognized: they were the first two hieroglyphs of the Secret.

For what...? Lord Pharaoh's question echoed in Cass's ear... *For what?... Why?*

She had thought the first two words of the Secret were *because what*, but what if a better translation was *for what*? That is to say, *why*. Why hadn't she seen that before?

Suddenly, it struck her: all along, she'd simply assumed that the Secret was the answer to all of life's mysteries, but the Secret wasn't an answer at all. The Secret was a question.

Or was it just that to find the answer, one first had to ask the question?

Max-Ernest and Yo-Yoji ran as fast as they could, huffing and puffing, until the stage came into view – along with all the complex machinery and sets and props one finds behind a stage of this size. Yo-Yoji stopped, seeing Lord Pharaoh's gold cape draped like a blanket over a chair. It would work for catching a bird, he thought. Why not a ghost?

Cass had had a breakthrough, but it had come too late. Suddenly, she felt overwhelmed by the hopelessness of her situation. Question or answer, it no longer mattered what the Secret was, because Lord Pharaoh was going to learn it first.

Where were her friends? she wondered in despair. Were they imprisoned in canopic jars, too?

"With this ring, your ring, the Ring of Thoth, we take back this man's life." As Lord Pharaoh pronounced these words, the gold ring appeared to float through the air until it reached the tip of the mummy's gold finger. "Live again, Doctor, live—"

"Hey, Lord Pharaoh, remember me?"

Yo-Yoji came running out of the wings, holding Lord Pharaoh's gold cape behind him. When he reached the centre of the stage, he threw the cape into the air. It didn't drop very far before landing on what was clearly Lord Pharaoh's head. Now the invisible magician was visible – albeit looking a bit like a badly costumed ghost on Halloween.

The audience applauded before the applause track could even roll. It was a great effect.

"Aah!" Lord Pharaoh cried in surprise. They could hear him stumble.

"Kiyah!" Before Lord Pharaoh could remove the

cape from his head, Yo-Yoji threw his shoulder into the unseen enemy, tackling him to the floor. From the way Yo-Yoji grimaced, he must have hit Lord Pharaoh rather hard. But Yo-Yoji recovered, pinning Lord Pharaoh to the stage while Max-Ernest ran up to them.

"Let go, you cretin!" Lord Pharaoh growled.

"Not a chance," said Yo-Yoji.

On the stage and off, guards and audience and dancers alike watched in confusion, unable to tell what was planned and what wasn't.

But Lord Pharaoh refused to call for help. Instead he shouted, "All part of the show, Ladies and Gentlemen! Take a bow, young sirs."

Max-Ernest quickly bowed, his mind racing. Clearly, Lord Pharaoh didn't want to cause an alarm. But why? Max-Ernest wondered. Then he realized: the mummy was stolen property. Lord Pharaoh didn't want security officers sniffing around the stage any more than Max-Ernest and his friends did. If the authorities were tipped off, they might confiscate the mummy before Lord Pharaoh had his way with it. Well, that was all to the good – Lord Pharaoh's concern worked to the trio's advantage.

Meanwhile, the wily ghost, still caught in the cape, was wriggling beneath Yo-Yoji on the floor. The invisible chocolate in his hand, Max-Ernest crouched down beside them. He pulled the cape off Lord Pharaoh's head. Then he felt around for Lord Pharaoh's face.

"Aaargh!" Lord Pharaoh grunted. "You two are going to pay."

Wincing with distaste, Max-Ernest prised Lord Pharaoh's mouth open with his fingers. He tried not to think about what Lord Pharaoh's teeth must look like; dental hygiene was not very advanced in the sixteenth century.

"Help me keep his mouth open," he said to Yo-Yoji. "Here..." Max-Ernest guided Yo-Yoji's hand to Lord Pharaoh's mouth.

"This is disgusting," complained Yo-Yoji, keeping his hand in place despite Lord Pharaoh's struggling.

"Eat," said Max-Ernest, forcing the invisible chocolate into the mouth of the invisible alchemist. "Ouch!" Lord Pharaoh had bitten down hard on Max-Ernest's finger. Instinctively, Max-Ernest pulled his hand away, but as far as he could tell, there was still some chocolate in Lord Pharaoh's mouth. And it didn't take much, he knew.

The Skelton Sisters were frantic. They shouted at the six gold musclemen standing onstage like statues.

"Do something!" "Hello – are you guys deaf?!"

The dancers blinked, uncertain whether to move.

Still hunched over Lord Pharaoh, Yo-Yoji and Max-

Ernest could feel the alchemist's body convulsing under the cape.

"I think…I think…it's working," said Max-Ernest.

First Lord Pharaoh's legs, then his arms, seemed to melt into the stage. By the time one of the dancers broke ranks and ran towards him, it was too late. There was nothing left where Lord Pharaoh had been – only a satin cape lying flat on the floor.

The audience applauded madly.

"Nice work, bro," said Yo-Yoji, breathing hard.

"Wha-what happened?" asked the dancer, sweat destroying his gold make-up.

"He went home," said Max-Ernest.

And it was true: Lord Pharaoh was now a problem for another age.

The Skelton Sisters screamed. "Antoinette!!" Then they ran off the stage.

Max-Ernest looked up to a box-style balcony on the side of the theatre just in time to see a flash of blonde hair and a shimmering gown. How long had Ms. Mauvais been there? In a blink, she was gone.

For good, Max-Ernest hoped.

In the melee, the brawny dancers who had been watching over Cass rushed to the centre of the stage, letting go of the jar that confined her. How to get out? She felt around, but the jar was locked from the outside. She had an idea, however. Although the jar was painted gold, she could tell by its texture that it was pottery. She wriggled around, rocking the jar until it fell to the floor with a crash. Ow! The pottery sides broke, just as she'd hoped they would, leaving her a bit banged up but free.

Cass scanned the area around where Lord Pharaoh had been. At first, she didn't see what she was looking for. Then – there it was, right at the foot of the mummy.

She darted across the stage and lunged for the ring.

The monocle was lying nearby. For good measure, she pocketed it, too.

"Cass!" her friends called out to her, but Cass didn't hear them. She was already standing in front of the mummy.

The ring fitted perfectly on the mummy's golden finger.

As Cass slipped it over the knuckle, the ring seemed to lock in place, sending sparks flying in all directions. She saw a flash of lightning bright enough to illuminate the entire auditorium, but – strangely – most of the room stayed dark. The noise of the theatre receded. The lights around her blurred. She felt as if she were in a tunnel. A tunnel with only two people in it. The mummy and herself. Facing each other.

And then, for a moment, she was in the sky. Flying. Over a great river. The Nile.

The ibis, she thought.

Then she was in the tunnel with the mummy again. The mummy's eyes blinked open. His dark, three-thousand-year-old eyes. They looked directly at Cassandra.

Death was staring her in the face.

Suddenly, Cass was afraid. Deeply afraid.

What had she done? She'd put the ring on the mummy's finger almost by instinct, without thinking. Why? Because Dr. L had told her she would learn the Secret? What if that was just another trap? The final trap?

Yes, she thought feverishly, that was what everything had been leading towards – the sacrifice of Cassandra. The mummy was going to kill her. He was going to turn her into one of his own. And not only her. You cannot bring death to life without bringing death *into* life. He was a demon whom she had unleashed on the world.

She gave herself a little shake and forced herself

to breathe. She had come too far – much too far – not to try to learn the Secret.

Because what ibis/Thoth river/Nile walk… Why ibis river walk…why ibis walk Nile…why ibis cross river…

Cass looked the mummy in the eye and carefully pronounced the words she'd been trying for so long to form in her mind. The words fell into place as she spoke them, as if they'd been there – somewhere – all along.

"Why did the ibis cross the Nile?"

The mummy stared at her, his ancient eyes seeming to penetrate her very being. For a second, she thought she'd asked the wrong question. Or that he had not regained the power of speech. Or that he was simply unwilling to answer.

He opened his mouth. Inside was only darkness.

Cass felt sick with despair. Why had she assumed this creature from ancient Egypt would understand her, or she him? Why had she assumed he could speak at all?

Then, in a voice so deep it seemed to come not from the mouth of a man, or even a mummy, but from the mouth of a volcano, a voice that would rattle buildings, shake mountains, the mummy repeated her question: "Why did the ibis cross the Nile?"

She nodded, shivering.

He laughed, a deep, rumbling laugh.

"To get to the other side, of course."

As Cass stared, frozen with fear, the laughter grew louder and louder, until it shook his entire body. Then, with a final shudder, he closed his eyes. The Ring of Thoth rattled on his finger and fell to the floor. Once again, the mummy was nothing but a pile of ragged cloth and dusty bones.

And for the first time in her still-young life, Cass fainted.

Show Time!

A joke?" Cass murmured. "It was all a joke?"

Yo-Yoji and Max-Ernest were crouched over their friend, just as they had been crouched over their enemy only a moment earlier.

They breathed matching sighs of relief. She was going to be fine.

"What's a joke?" asked Max-Ernest.

"What? Oh. Nothing," said Cass, forcing herself awake. "I guess I was dreaming. Are we still on the stage?"

"Yep, you were only out for a second," said Yo-Yoji, helping her to her feet.

No longer worried about Cass, Max-Ernest glanced around the stage. The Skelton Sisters were gone, as were all Midnight Sun members, as far as he could tell. The gold-painted dancers stared at them, picking at the gems glued inside their belly buttons, not sure what to do. Audience members spoke to one another in nervous whispers, uncertain whether the spectacle had been planned or not. Even the guards in the aisles seemed confused. But it would only be a matter of seconds before the guards – and everybody else – wised up.

The friends needed time to get away, thought Max-Ernest.

But what to do?

Max-Ernest heard a clinking sound and looked down. One of Cass's two remaining gold coins – it must have fallen out of her pocket. He picked it up off the floor.

Suddenly, he had an inspiration. This was a magic show, wasn't it? And what did people always say – the show must go on?

"You guys get out of here," he whispered to Cass and Yo-Yoji. "I'll distract everyone. Meet you outside in a minute."

Shakily, Max-Ernest got to his feet – and found himself alone in the middle of the biggest stage that he'd ever seen, let alone set foot on.

"Hi, er, Ladies and Gentlemen. It is I…the real Lord Pharaoh," Max-Ernest shouted, trying to match Lord Pharaoh's Old World accent. The effect was not entirely authentic; he sounded like a small child speaking into a Darth Vader style voice-changing microphone.

He stepped to the front of the stage. From this vantage point, the room looked huge and dark. He hadn't realized quite how many people were there. And they were all watching him! "Think of me as that little man standing behind Lord Pharaoh's curtain – you know, like in *The Wizard of Oz*?"

If he was expecting a warm reception, he didn't get it. The audience jeered:

"Yeah, right!" *"Very funny, kid, sit down!"* *"Somebody call his parents, please!"*

"Don't believe me? I'll prove it to you." He held the gold coin above his head.

Max-Ernest's image appeared on the big screen behind him. The cameraman, wherever he was, had decided to play along.

"I am Lord Pharaoh, the greatest alchemist of all time!" Max-Ernest tried to keep his voice steady. "I have in my hand a gold coin. Watch, and I shall make it disappear—"

This should be easy, Max-Ernest thought. He was going to do a simple sleight-of-hand trick that all magicians know, one that Pietro had shown him numerous times. But his hand was shaking with nervousness. And when he tried to slip the coin between his fingers –

– it dropped onto the stage.

The audience was predictably merciless:

"Boo!" *"Go home!"* *"You said you'd make it disappear, not drop it!"*

As he picked up the coin, he felt about as low as he possibly could. Where was the applause track when you really needed it? At that very second, he wanted to jump off the stage and run from the theatre, but he told himself he had to stay where he was. He stole a look at the golden dancers, restless at the side of the stage. Most likely, Cass and Yo-Yoji wouldn't have been able to make it all the way out of the hotel yet. He had to buy them just a little more time.

When he stood up, he did his best to smile like a boy who knew exactly what he was doing. "Of course I didn't make it disappear!" he said gamely. "Would *you* want to make a gold coin disappear? No, you'd want to keep it!"

There were a few laughs and a few jeers. Mostly jeers. But one person shouted, "Oh, give the kid a chance – he's kinda funny!"

That gave Max-Ernest an idea: if he couldn't do magic, he would try to make the audience laugh – at him or with him, either would have to do.

"Okay, I know I'm not the only magician around here. So who knows this one? How many magicians does it take to change a light bulb?"

He waited just long enough for the question to sink in before answering it: "Well, that depends on what you want the light bulb to change into!"

I'll admit there were more than a few groans, but I also submit that there were a few laughs. So it wasn't the greatest joke in the world. Or the newest. What light-bulb joke is? For Max-Ernest, at the time, it represented progress. He didn't even try to explain the joke after he told it.

And then Max-Ernest had a little moment of comic inspiration; he made up a joke on the spot, as opposed to merely repeating one he'd read. "But the real question is, how many light bulbs does it take to change a magician?" he said.

After a beat, he answered, "I'm not sure exactly, but tonight a light bulb went off in my head, and I realized I'm not much of magician anyway. So I changed into a comedian."

This time he got a real laugh. And he learned an important lesson: when in doubt, make fun of yourself. Self-deprecating humour is the surest kind.

"And just now another light bulb went off in my head." He paused. "I bet you thought I was going to say I'm not a comedian, either, huh? But actually, all I meant was that it's time for me to go."

It had been about three minutes – enough time, he hoped, for Cass and Yo-Yoji to get out of the hotel.

Max-Ernest smiled and bowed. "And now, if you'll excuse me –"

While the audience watched in confusion, he leaped off the stage, ran up the aisle, and exited the theatre.

Which really is the most legitimate sort of disappearing trick, don't you agree?

Chapter Thirty-Three

The Priests of Amun

Thcy hadn't agreed on a meeting place. How often had it been drilled into their heads? By parents and Terces Society leaders alike. Make sure you decide on a meeting place. And yet they hadn't done so.

When he got out of the hotel, he looked around, vaguely hoping he would see his friends, but he feared they were long gone by now – either on the way to a bus station or in the hands of the Midnight Sun.

As he stood hesitating, wondering whether he should stay or go, he gradually realized that the eye of the Egyptian-style "living statue" nearest to him kept twitching – seemingly winking at Max-Ernest. Seeing Max-Ernest glance at him, the statue started shaking his head ever so slightly.

Max-Ernest looked at him questioningly. Was he trying to tell Max-Ernest something?

The statue kept shaking his head, but it must have been obvious that Max-Ernest had no clue what he was trying to communicate. Finally, he beckoned Max-Ernest closer with a slight movement of his index finger.

Max-Ernest walked over nervously. Was he finally going to hear from the Midnight Sun? The man wasn't wearing gloves, but his hands weren't bare, either – they were covered in make-up. Perhaps that was enough.

"Somebody across the street's been waving to you for the last three minutes, you blind idiot!" he said through gritted teeth, then quickly re-froze in his statue pose.

"Oh. Thanks."

Max-Ernest looked across the street, expecting to see Cass or Yo-Yoji. Instead, he was greeted by a very peculiar sight: the Priests of Amun, no longer carrying their signs, now sitting on motorcycles. They wore colourful motorcycle helmets over their turbans, and black motorcycle boots under their robes.

Two of the priests now had passengers riding behind them, also wearing helmets. Max-Ernest recognized Cass and Yo-Yoji by their clothes. His heart skipped a beat. His friends had been kidnapped! Well, it was only a matter of time. He knew they'd all escaped too easily.

The third biker-priest motioned impatiently for him to join them.

Quickly, Max-Ernest examined his options. If he made a run for it – and managed to escape – he could try to contact Pietro and get help. But he wouldn't know where the priests had taken his friends – or where to go to rescue them. Besides, what were the chances he could outrun three men on motorcycles? If he went with them willingly, however, he and his friends might find a better moment to escape later that night. And the three of them working together would improve the odds of success.

He ran across the street.

"Get on, sahib!" said the priest gruffly from under his helmet. His Arabic accent was thick.

"No, let my friends go!" said Max-Ernest. He knew he sounded foolish, but he figured it couldn't hurt to put up a little bit of a fight.

"Sorry – they're coming. You can stay or go." The priest gunned the bike's motor as if he were about to leave.

"Who are you?" asked Max-Ernest, stalling. "The Priests of Amun – is that, like, some secret cult descended from ancient Egypt?"

The biker coughed under the helmet. "You could say that."

Max-Ernest gagged. So it was true – they were an ancient order of vengeful Egyptians. Who knew what kind of strange ritual tortures they planned!

"We didn't do it! We didn't touch the mummy," said Max-Ernest in a rush. "It was Lord Pharaoh!"

"We know."

"You do?" Max-Ernest looked at him in surprise. "You're not really the Priests of Amun, are you?"

The man shook his head.

"I knew there was something off about you guys. Now that I think of it, Amun isn't even the mummy's real name! It's just a pseudonym the museum gave him. So how could there be Priests of Amun?"

"You got me."

Max-Ernest eyed the bikers' motorcycle gloves, an awful realization overtaking him. "You're the Midnight Sun!"

The biker laughed. "No, that we're not, but I'm sure they'll be here any second, if you want to wait."

A passenger on one of the other bikes lifted his helmet: it was Yo-Yoji. "Just get on, dude!" he shouted.

The other passenger lifted her helmet: Cass. "They're taking us home, silly!"

"They are?" Astonished, Max-Ernest looked from his friends to the priest in front of him. "You are? Are you sure you didn't threaten them to make them say that?"

"If I wanted to kidnap you, you'd already be kidnapped," said the priest, lifting his visor and losing his accent at the same time. "Now get on the bike already—"

"Owen?!"

"Yes, doofus."

Max-Ernest reddened. "Don't call me that," he said, climbing onto the seat behind Owen. He couldn't believe he had thought Owen was an ancient Egyptian priest – he knew he was never going to live it down.

"Is that your way of saying 'thanks for rescuing me'?" asked Owen, chuckling.

"No, it's my way of saying 'where were you when we needed you in the theatre'?"

"Playing blackjack – what do you think? I knew you guys could handle it."

Max-Ernest slipped, then pulled himself back onto the bike, trying not to think about the trip ahead. (I probably don't have to tell you that this was his first time on a motorcycle.) He hoped Owen's motorcycle riding was smoother than his car driving, but he had a sneaking suspicion that it wasn't.

In front of them, the other two bikes were already pulling out into traffic.

"Who's driving those ones?" asked Max-Ernest.

"Mickey and Morrie."

"The clowns!? No wonder you were playing blackjack. I'm surprised you ever got them out of the casino."

"Here, wear this –" Owen handed Max-Ernest a helmet like the ones the others were wearing.

"Cass's mom is going to kill her," said Max-Ernest, putting on the helmet. "She *hates* motorcycles. She works in the insurance industry, so she knows all about accident statistics."

Owen chuckled. "Hold on!"

"*Wait!*"

"What?"

"Somebody's got to call Albert 3-D and tell him the mummy's waiting for him onstage."

"Already done. He's on the way." Owen revved his engine, and suddenly Max-Ernest's head whipped backwards.

Just as Max-Ernest was about to sail off the back of the bike, he reached around Owen's waist and gripped his priestly robe. Max-Ernest's palms were sweaty. He could feel the wind rushing by. They were off.

And he was terrified.

To calm his mind, he started counting down in his head. But that only made him think of rocket ships taking off – and the high likelihood of launch explosions. He tried to imagine a peaceful forest scene instead, but in a flash, his forest was consumed by fire – a fire sparked, of course, by a motorcycle accident on a mountain highway.

And yet, he reminded himself, as long as he was afraid, he was still alive. But then why was it so dark? It took him a few seconds to realize that his eyes were closed. Tentatively, he opened them –

The brilliant lights of the Vegas Strip passed by in a dizzying blur – as if they had entered warp speed and were shooting through entire galaxies in a matter of seconds.

A moment later, they were flying through the cold, dark desert.

This is what it must feel like to be abducted by aliens, he thought.

Terrifying, yes. But grand.

He wouldn't have traded it for the world.

CHAPTER THIRTY-FOUR

Chicken

What a difference a day and a returned mummy make.

The trio's reception at home wasn't at all what they'd expected. Rather than being "grounded for life", as they'd predicted, Yo-Yoji and Cass and Max-Ernest were greeted like returning war heroes.

It seemed everybody (meaning mostly their parents) accepted their story about being kidnapped at gunpoint by that villainous magician known as Lord Pharaoh. If he was capable of stealing a mummy, all agreed, why *wouldn't* he wrap three kids in linen bandages, throw them into a sarcophagus, and ship them to Las Vegas with only cat food to sustain them? (You will notice that our creative young runaways threw a few reality-based elements into this rather heavily embroidered story.) As for his current whereabouts, Lord Pharaoh was believed to have fled north to Canada under the protection of a ruthless gang of bikers with ties to the Egyptian mafia. The erstwhile Vegas entertainer was now the subject of a nationwide police manhunt.

Most surprising of all was the greeting they received at school. When they arrived Friday morning, after having missed two days of school, a smiling Mrs. Johnson stood in front of the school gates under a giant banner painted to look like a movie poster.

Return of the Mummy
The Defeat of Lord Pharaoh
Starring
Cass, Max-Ernest and Yo-Yoji

As was clear from the paint all over his clothes, if not from the grin on his face, Daniel-not-Danielle had created the banner. And not a bad job, he had done, too. (Perhaps in the future, comic-book illustration would be his *thing*.) Even Glob gave them a thumbs up.

With cameras flashing, Mrs. Johnson welcomed them back, telling them they were heroes and a credit to their "institution of higher, er, middle school learning".

Now, a sceptic might say that it was the presence of journalists that had turned Mrs. Johnson into such a warm and sunny principal. (Like most people in her profession, Mrs. Johnson was very sensitive to the way her school was portrayed in the media.) However, in her defence, after the cameras had left and there were no longer any witnesses, Mrs. Johnson did not suddenly turn back into her old sourpuss self.

On the contrary, she told her surprised students that she had a special, private congratulatory present for the three of them to share.

"It hasn't felt right since you returned it. I just don't think it belongs to me any more," said Mrs. Johnson, taking a familiar Aztec artefact out of her purse. "Who would like to be responsible for this?"

The boys looked at Cass, and Mrs. Johnson handed her the Tuning Fork.

As official mummy-rescuing heroes, Cass and Max-Ernest were allowed to go where they wished on a Saturday afternoon without having to employ the least bit of subterfuge. They merely told their parents that they were getting together for a walk.

True, Cass's mother did volunteer something about not wanting her daughter to be kidnapped again, but Cass pointed out that if she could escape from a mad magician, she could escape from anyone. Besides, she couldn't live her whole life in fear of being nabbed and taken (or, rather, shut up in a box and mailed) to Las Vegas, could she? And true, Max-Ernest, who was once again the apple of his parents' very separate eyes, had to promise both his mother and father individually that he would spend the next Saturday afternoon with them, but he managed to get out of the house without even his baby brother crawling after him.

The walk was not quite as cheery as it sounds, however. Cass, at least, remained rather sullen most of the way to the circus. Occasionally, her ears would flare red, and it looked as though she might be about to say something, but Max-Ernest hardly noticed. As was often the case, he was speaking enough for the two of them:

"...or what about starting with a joke that goes like this: 'Sorry, I was going to bring my graduation speech today, really, I swear, but my dog ate it this morning...' Get it? It's a joke on the classic line 'the dog ate my homework', or 'the cat ate my homework', or whatever, only it's the dog ate my graduation speech—"

"Huh?" Cass was paying little attention – so little, in fact, that she accidentally put a questioning inflection at the end of her "huh", which made Max-Ernest explain himself (rather than continuing to babble on without bothering her too much with what he was saying, as she would have preferred).

"Do you like the joke? It's my favourite kind, the joke on the joke. I made it up from scratch. I didn't even read it in a book. I'm writing all my own material now. All the best comics do. Although even the best guys sometimes buy jokes. Did you know you can sell jokes to comedians for fifty dollars each? How 'bout that?"

Who knew that a single turn on a Vegas stage could do so much for one fledgling comedian's confidence. And yet there was no doubt that Max-Ernest had a new humorous spring in his step, a comic twinkle in his eye, that he'd never had before. He didn't just look funny; the possibility existed, for the very first time, that he might *be* funny.

Cass, however, was immune to the charms of the new Max-Ernest. She looked at him darkly. "Don't talk to me about jokes."

"But the speech is due tomorrow! If I don't figure out the joke now, when will I?"

Cass's ears glowed red. "Don't. Talk. About. Jokes."

"Uh, okay," said Max-Ernest, taken aback by the fierceness of her tone.

"I *hate* jokes!"

"Okay. We won't talk about them."

"Good." She walked ahead.

"You didn't used to hate them," said Max-Ernest nervously, following behind her. "I mean, you didn't like *my* jokes. But that was because you didn't think they were funny or because I didn't tell them right. Not because you hated jokes in general—"

"That was before."

"Before what?"

Cass gave him a look.

"You mean with the mummy?"

Cass didn't say anything.

"That means yes." Max-Ernest was not always very astute about non-verbal clues, but in this case Cass's meaning was clear.

Earlier that day, Max-Ernest had tried to press Cass for details about what transpired onstage between her and the mummy, but she wouldn't tell him anything. He knew she had tried to put the ring on the mummy – he'd seen that much. But he didn't know whether she had learned the Secret. It was quite strange, really; his memory of the moment was a total blur. All he knew for certain was that Cass had been in a terrible mood ever since then.

"What does the mummy have to do with jokes?" he asked.

"It's not the mummy himself; it's what he said."

Max-Ernest stared at his friend in surprise. "He spoke to you?"

She nodded.

"In English?"

"Uh-huh. Well, I think so."

"Wouldn't he speak Egyptian? If he were going to speak. English wasn't even invented when he was alive."

She hesitated. She hadn't necessarily meant to talk to Max-Ernest about this. But now that she was talking to him, she had to admit it was a big relief.

"It was kind of like a dream," she said. "I mean, I don't know if the mummy was really talking or if it was more like telepathy. Or maybe he was talking in Egyptian and somehow what he said got magically translated in my brain...?"

Max-Ernest looked dubious. "On a purely statistical basis, all those things are pretty unlikely."

"Well, *something* happened. I heard him talk to me."

"Okay, let's say – hypothetically – that you heard him talk to you," said Max-Ernest, humouring her. "What does that have to do with jokes?"

"Well, I guess you could say he told one."

"The mummy told you a joke?" Max-Ernest was incredulous.

She nodded.

"So he didn't tell you the you-know-what?"

"No, well, yes, I mean, that's what it was..."

Max-Ernest blinked in astonishment. This was a possibility – one of the few – that he had never contemplated. "The you-know-what is a joke?"

Cass nodded unhappily.

"A *joke* joke or a joke as in, *that's so dumb, it's a joke*."

"A *joke* joke."

"A *joke* joke?"

Cass nodded. "A joke you know."

Max-Ernest, the joke lover, was appalled. "The you-know-what, the thing that nobody is supposed to know, the thing that we've done all those things for, the thing that you went back in time to find out – you're saying that thing is a joke I already know?"

Cass nodded.

"Now *you're* joking, right?"

"I wish I were," said Cass.

"So what was the joke?"

"You know I can't tell you."

"But you said I knew the joke already!" Max-Ernest protested. "Just give me a hint, at least."

Cass looked at him. What's the difference? she thought glumly. "Think chicken."

"Chicken, as in *scared*?"

"A *chicken* chicken."

"A scared chicken?"

"No. Just a chicken!"

Max-Ernest looked nonplussed. "A joke about a chicken. The you-know-what is a joke about a chicken."

"Uh-huh."

"A story joke or a riddle?"

"Riddle."

Max-Ernest thought for a second, trying to absorb this new and thoroughly distressing piece of information. Then his eyes widened. "Is it a famous riddle?"

Cass nodded.

"Like, really famous?"

Cass nodded.

Max-Ernest shook his head. "Really? *That* is the... you-know-what?"

Cass nodded. "Yeah. That's it. Only substitute *ibis* for *chicken*."

"I can't believe it! I thought... well, I thought a lot of things. But nothing like that. It doesn't make any sense!"

"I know. I couldn't believe it, either."

"Well, so what's the answer?"

"What do you mean?"

"What's the answer? Which is it?"

"Which is what?" asked Cass, totally confused.

"Which came first – the ibis or the egg?"

Cass put her head in her hands. "Not *that* chicken joke!"

There was no time for her to clear up the matter, however; they had reached Pietro's trailer.

Cass could see Yo-Yoji's bicycle parked next to one of the tents nearby. Inside, she could hear Lily Wei shouting instructions. "Kiyah!" Yo-Yoji responded. He was practising martial arts. It seemed almost sad, Cass thought, to hear the two of them working at it all so seriously, now that she knew the Secret was nothing more than, well, what it was.

For the hundredth time, Cass tried not to think about it. If the Secret was a joke, did that mean the whole Terces Society was? Pietro and everyone? The Jester? The homunculus?

Was she a joke, too?

The
Other Side

Pietro's trailer was small and simply furnished, with a cot-size bed, a card table and a sink and mini-refrigerator for a kitchen.

The only personal touch was an old, banged-up bureau – painted with dragons and other chinoiserie* – that looked as though it had travelled the world, as indeed it had. On top sat Pietro's top hat, which was looking a bit past its prime; the hat tilted to the side as if engaged in conversation with an invisible partner.

Pietro was sitting at the card table when they entered. His eyes were red, and his hair and moustache were even more bedraggled than usual. It looked as though he hadn't slept. On the table in front of him were an old circus ticket, a playbill advertising the Bergamo Brothers, and the mandolin-rose vial that Dr. L had given him – the last remaining scent instrument from the Symphony of Smells.

He smiled at the sight of the young Terces members. "Ah, Cassandra, Max-Ernest, I forgot you were coming," he said, standing. "I should make some espresso?"

---

*Chinoiserie means Chinese – or, more accurately, Chinese things – in French. The word usually refers to things that look Chinese in style, though they are not truly Chinese. Just as this footnote looks like it contains useful information, though it truly does not.

"That's okay," said Max-Ernest. "We don't really drink espresso."

"Oh, right – I forget. You are still so young."

"But if there's more hot chocolate—"

Cass cut him off. "You can have hot chocolate later."

All business, Cass pushed aside the circus ticket and the playbill. Then she opened her backpack and laid three objects on the table in front of Pietro: the Tuning Fork, the Double Monocle and the Ring of Thoth.

Pietro raised a bushy eyebrow. "Aha. Well done. Mr. Wallace, he will be very happy. He will put these things in the archive along with the Sound Prism and the last vial of the Symphony of Smells. There they can do no more mischief, I hope." His eyes twinkled briefly. "Unless you steal them back again."

"Taste. Sight. Touch. Hearing. Smell." Max-Ernest folded his arms. "One object for every sense."

Pietro smiled at him. "Very astute."

There was an awkward silence. They were all standing; Pietro had not asked his guests to sit down.

He looked at them with heavy eyes. "Is there anything else?"

"Uh…" Max-Ernest didn't know what to say. The question was so unlike Pietro. Usually, Pietro was almost as chatty as Max-Ernest was, but it seemed very much that he was trying to end the visit.

"Yeah, there is," said Cass stiffly. "I have to ask you something, and I want you to tell me the truth."

"I always tell the truth, when I can."

"When you made us swear the Oath of Terces, when you told me I was the Secret Keeper and finding out the Secret was the most important thing in the world, when we were fighting the Midnight Sun all that time..." She broke off, trembling. It was almost too hard to say.

"Yes?"

"Did you know the you-know-what—?" She stopped herself; what was the use of hiding the name any more? "Did you know the Secret was a joke?" she spat out.

"I'm sorry – I don't understand," said Pietro.

"Well, I don't understand, either!" declared Cass. Angrily, she started describing her experience with the mummy.

Pietro raised his hand just before she could tell him what the mummy said. "Please, do not repeat his words. You know the Secret has power."

"Why? It's just a joke. It doesn't mean anything."

"You are so sure?"

Cass laughed derisively. "So you still think it's serious? You wouldn't if you knew it."

The old magician shrugged. "Maybe. Or maybe those things – the joke and the serious – they are not always so different as you might think."

Max-Ernest looked confused. "That doesn't make sense. Something serious and a joke, they're opposites." In all his studies of jokes, this was one conclusion he considered incontrovertible. As far as he was concerned, his problem in the past was that he had taken jokes far too seriously.

"Think about it – if the Secret is a joke, it is not only a joke," said Pietro. "Or put it another way: if the biggest secret in the world is a joke, jokes must be a lot more important than you thought."

"I still don't understand," said Cass.

"I know, Cassandra, and I am sorry. But can we please continue this conversation another time. It is very important, yes, but..." He trailed off. There were tears in his eyes.

"What is it? What's wrong?" As mad as Cass was, it made her uneasy to see the old magician cry. It took the self-righteous *umph* out of her anger.

"It is my brother."

"Dr. L? What did he do now?" asked Max-Ernest. "Is he mad because we got out of his trap?"

"He has done nothing. He has died."

"Oh," said Max-Ernest.

He and Cass were silent. As you know, fatal illnesses and disasters were their respective specialities. But death itself left them speechless.

"After you two saw him, my brother, he stopped taking those evil elixirs," explained Pietro. "I think he wanted to prove to me he was true – he was done with the Midnight Sun. He came for a last visit and looked very old, very old. He could hardly to speak. And then this morning – he is no more." His eyes filled again with tears. "I only wish that I'd had the chance to tell him I knew he had changed, I knew he was sorry. I hate to think that he left me, not knowing that I believed him. That I forgave him."

"I guess you still loved him a lot," Cass ventured.

Pietro nodded and opened the door for them. The visit was over.

"Do not worry too much for me. I will see him again soon, I am sure," said Pietro, ushering them out.

Cass stopped short. She looked stricken. "You're not . . . dying, too?"

"Oh no," he said reassuringly. "I meant on *l'altro lato*."

"Where's that?" asked Max-Ernest. "Is that in Italy?"

Pietro smiled through his tears. "It's everywhere. And nowhere. It's the place you cannot touch. *L'altro lato*. The other side."

He closed the door with a tad more force than perhaps he intended.

Cass and Max-Ernest stood outside the trailer, their brains churning.

"The other side..." Max-Ernest repeated, turning to Cass. "The other side. That's the answer, isn't it? I mean, that's the Secret, er, the riddle, I mean, that's the chicken joke! Not 'Which came first, the chicken or the egg?' It's 'Why did the chicken cross the road? To get to the other side.' How could I not have thought of that?"

But Cass didn't answer. She was lost in her own thoughts, Pietro's words still reverberating in her head as well.

The other side...the other side...

Perhaps Pietro was right, and the mummy wasn't telling a joke, she thought. Or not *only* a joke.

"What if the joke's not the whole Secret," said Cass in a rush. "What if the Secret *is* the other side. Or how to get to the other side. Or maybe even something *on* the other side."

"What are you saying? I just figured out the joke, and now you're saying that it's not the Secret after all!" Max-Ernest couldn't help being a little irritated.

"No, it is, yeah, but also it isn't," said Cass. "Think about it – all this time, we've been looking for the Secret, we've seen so many things. I mean, the homunculus, where did he come from? Señor Hugo's chocolate, where did that take me? There's been some secret place...or dimension or something... all along."

"The other side?" Max-Ernest tried to understand what she was saying.

"I've got to tell him I know what he means. I was all mad about something I had no reason to be mad about."

She knocked on the trailer door. "Pietro?"

There was no answer.

"Pietro, please. I want to apologize."

There was still no answer. Cass and Max-Ernest looked at each other.

"Pietro, are you okay?"

Worried, Cass opened the door and cautiously stepped inside. She took in the room at a glance. Pietro was nowhere to be seen.

Max-Ernest looked in after her. "Where'd he go?"

Everything in the trailer was just as they'd left it – except Pietro's top hat. It was now lying in the middle of the linoleum floor, as though it had been carelessly tossed and forgotten. Max-Ernest picked it up and put it on his head. It fitted perfectly (and he still has it to this day).

They looked around. There was almost nowhere to hide except under the bed; and there was nothing there but balls of dust.

"This is really weird. There's no way he could have come out without us seeing him."

"He's a magician," said Max-Ernest, peeking behind and beneath Pietro's old chinoiserie bureau. "I'm sure there are all kinds of hidden doors and hatches in this place – in the floor, in the ceiling." He opened drawers; they were full of scarves, balls, dice, coins. "Pietro is expert at all that stuff."

"You think?" Cass wasn't convinced.

Max-Ernest nodded, waving one of Pietro's wands. "He probably just snuck out the bottom of the trailer and then…presto!…he ran off without us seeing him. How 'bout that?"

"Then why don't we see the opening now?"

"A magician never reveals his tricks."

"Why trick us at all? He could have just waited for us to leave."

"Um…" Max-Ernest didn't have a good answer.

"Look," said Cass, picking up the Ring of Thoth off the floor. "It must have been hidden under the top hat."

As she turned the ring over in her hand, she felt a familiar buzz. What was it about the touch of this ring that was so powerful? Perhaps, on some level, the ring was a gag, as Max-Ernest had once suggested. But it was also something more. It had brought a mummy to life. What might it have done to Pietro?

"I know what you're thinking," said Max-Ernest, seeing the expression on her face. "You're thinking he put the hat on and then the ring and he just—"

"Went *poof*? Yes."

Max-Ernest shook his head. "Remember the last time he disappeared – when we first met?" They'd thought he went up in a puff of smoke in his kitchen, but it was a trick.

Cass disagreed. This time, she thought, Pietro had truly disappeared. He had gone somewhere else. *L'altro lato.* The other side.

And she was confident that if she needed to, she could find him there.

But she didn't say anything to Max-Ernest. He didn't need to believe it if he didn't want to. The other side was her secret – *the* Secret.

She was the Secret Keeper.

CHAPTER
THIRTY-
SIX

On the Road

One month later

"Grandpa Larry! Grandpa Wayne!"

Cass ran into her grandfathers' arms, her graduation cap falling off her head.

"I didn't know you were back."

"Surprise!" Grandpa Larry grinned. "We wouldn't miss this for the world."

"We got in this morning," said Grandpa Wayne. "We didn't even have time to shower."

Cass wrinkled her nose. "I can tell." They all laughed.

"Actually, we didn't get very far – our money ran out," admitted Grandpa Larry cheerfully.

"Really? After everything you sold at the garage sale?" asked Cass, incredulous.

"Turns out we're not very good businessmen."

"Well, I could have told you that!" said Cass, who was wondering how many gold coins it would take to buy them a lifetime supply of cruise tickets.

Grandpa Wayne looked at Cass. "What's different about you? You look taller...more free..."

Grandpa Larry snapped his fingers. "She's not wearing her backpack!"

Cass shrugged sheepishly. "Well, I figured graduation was bound to be such a total disaster that nothing in my backpack would help."

As Larry and Wayne regaled her with stories – no doubt much exaggerated – about their adventures at sea, Cass's eyes wandered around the soccer field, where the rest of her classmates were greeting their friends and relatives.

Everybody was very dressed up – as if it weren't enough to graduate from middle school, they had to skip all the way to adulthood. It gave Cass a funny feeling, like she was looking off a precipice.

Yo-Yoji, who was sparring with his little brother while talking to his parents and sister, was wearing a dark, skinny suit that made him look like a mod British rocker from another era. Max-Ernest, who was looking back and forth between his parents like a referee at a tennis match, had tried to smooth his spiky hair with some kind of gel; it kept popping up – and he kept patting it down.

As for Cass, she wasn't in a dress – much to her mother's chagrin. She had consented to a skirt, however; and she'd had a second manicure, this time deep green – "as a statement", she said. But privately she admitted to herself that she rather liked the way it looked.

Amber, of course, looked the most polished; for her, dressing up was effortless. But she seemed oddly quiet. Rather than chatting and gossiping with Naomi and

Veronica, as she normally would, she was standing by her parents' side, her mind evidently elsewhere.

Cass was considering Amber's unusual behaviour, when she finally saw the person she was seeking. "Excuse me," she said to her grandfathers. "There's somebody I have to talk to."

Promising to spend more time with them after the ceremony, Cass ran across the field, glad she had refused her mother's suggestion of high heels.

She found her mother standing under the MUMMY RETURNS banner (now a bit tattered) with Albert 3-D and Daniel-not-Danielle.

Daniel-not-Danielle's dreads were tied back, exposing the whole of his face for the first time. For a second, Cass couldn't tell him apart from his father.

"Hey, Albert 3-D, I mean, Albert, I mean, Professor," said Cass, breathless.

The professor laughed. "Albert 3-D is fine. I can't seem to shake it."

"Even I call him that sometimes," said Daniel-not-Danielle.

"Well, anyway, I just wanted say, well, I never said I was sorry. I know I caused you a lot of trouble. I should never have touched the mummy, and then—"

Albert 3-D stopped her. "It's okay, Cass, I know you're sorry. And I'm grateful to you for finding the mummy. And for, well, a lot of things." He smiled at Cass's mom.

"Albert's a forgiving man – a very nice quality," said Cass's mother, smiling. "I'll bet sometimes you wish your mother were more like that – don't you, sweetie?"

As her mother spoke, Cass noticed that her mother's hand was grazing Albert 3-D's – for much longer than one would normally touch a fellow parent at school. In fact, if Cass didn't know better, she might have almost thought the touching was intentional. Yes, it must be – their pinkies were interlocked!

For a second, Cass locked eyes with the equally alarmed Daniel-not-Danielle. Was it possible their parents were having a romance? The idea was too icky to contemplate.

"Bye!" said Cass hurriedly. "It's almost time – we gotta get our seats."

On the other hand, she thought, as she and Daniel-not-Danielle scurried away, if her mother had to be involved with someone, there were worse choices than a Nigerian archaeologist. At least with him around, there was a chance they would get to travel...

* * *

"And now I am proud to present the winner of this year's Book-a-Day Reading Challenge, our very own Bookworm..."

Mrs. Johnson, resplendent in an apple-green hat and trouser suit, gestured to the still-short (but growing!) boy sitting in the front row next to Cass and Yo-Yoji.

"...Max-Ernest!"

Grinning from ear to ear, Max-Ernest stepped up to the podium and shook Mrs. Johnson's hand. Then he laid his speech down, looked at the microphone, and took a breath.

"Thank you, Principal Johnson," he began formally. "Greetings, Parents, Teachers, Fellow Classmates."

He had greased his hair back again, but as he spoke, it sprang back to its usual spiky state with an almost audible *boing*. He patted it down. "For the last few months—"

His hair sprang up again. There were a few giggles. He coughed. This was not an auspicious beginning.

After his stint on the big stage in Las Vegas, Max-Ernest had expected a mere middle-school graduation (or, as he thought of it now, a *gig*) to be no big deal. But looking out at all the people who had been characters in the story of his life for the last eight-odd years, he found himself unaccountably nervous.

"For the last few months," he began reading again, "I've been racking my brain trying to find the perfect joke to open this speech. Well, I think I came up with something that's going to really, really shock you."

The audience tittered nervously. A few teachers gave him warning looks. This was not the occasion for an off-colour joke.

"I'm not going to open with a joke at all."

Everybody laughed with relief.

"See, I told you it would be shocking." Max-Ernest looked up at the audience and smiled mischievously. "Well, now that I've opened without a joke, I'm going to tell a joke anyway. Bet you didn't see that coming!"

"No, don't do it, dude!" "Stop!" "Just say no!" his friends shouted good-naturedly.

"Kidding! I'm actually going to skip right to the serious part." He looked down at his speech again. "When I was younger, I had a lot of trouble relating to other kids. People who know me know that I didn't always understand my peers, and they didn't understand me. That's a polite way of saying they thought I was really annoying."

"We still do!" yelled Glob.

"See, and that's one of my best friends," said Max-Ernest. "Sometimes, I thought everybody else had a secret sense that I didn't have. Something besides the usual senses – smell, hearing, taste, sight and touch. A sixth sense, in other words. But what was that secret sense? I used to wonder. Telepathy? Seeing dead people? Was that what was really happening on the schoolyard all that time, so I didn't know what the other kids were talking about? They were seeing ghosts?"

The audience laughed. Cass and Yo-Yoji exchanged looks. The speech was getting a little too close to home.

"As most of you know, I like to tell jokes and riddles. A lot. I've always been interested in jokes, but I'm not sure I ever understood why. As I think about it now, though, I think jokes were my way of trying to learn or acquire this secret sense that other kids have. To me, the sixth sense is not something especially supernatural. It is something that binds us together as people. And makes us human. It's a sense of humour."

He paused to make sure he still had everybody's attention. He did.

"Friends don't have to have a lot of things in common. One of them might like, oh, solar flashlights. Another might like Day-Glo sneakers..."

He smiled at Cass and Yo-Yoji. Cass smiled back. Yo-Yoji gave him a thumbs up.

"Another might like chocolate. Lots of chocolate. I'm not naming names –" Casually, he pulled a chocolate bar out of his coat pocket, unwrapped it, and took a big bite.

There were more laughs – his biggest yet.

"But there's one thing friends usually do have in common – a sense of humour. That doesn't mean they have to find all the same things funny. Sometimes, they might even laugh at each other. But at the end of the day, friends can always laugh *with* each other."

Cass and Yo-Yoji turned to each other and smiled. Their friend was doing great. As they turned back, their hands accidentally brushed. Cass was shocked to find their pinkies interlocking – just the way her mother's and Albert 3-D's had! She froze, the blood rushing in her ears. Max-Ernest might have been speechifying about the sense of humour, but it was the sense of touch that now occupied Cass's attention.

After an agonizing moment, she and Yo-Yoji pulled away from each other.

"Are you still wearing that ring?" whispered Yo-Yoji, not looking at her.

"No. Why?" she whispered back, not just her ears but her whole face bright red with embarrassment.

"I just thought I felt, uh, a jolt or something. Never mind," said Yo-Yoji quickly.

"Quiet, lovebirds – your friend's talking," said Glob from the row behind them.

Daniel-not-Danielle giggled. "Yeah, show some respect."

Mortified, Cass and Yo-Yoji sat stiffly in their chairs, neither able to muster the slightest comeback.

Max-Ernest, meanwhile, had reached full stride. "The official theme of this speech is supposed to be 'The Secret of Success'," he said, with a nod towards Mrs. Johnson. "Well, I don't know if a sense of humour is the secret of success. So far, I haven't made a lot of money as a comedian. In fact, I've been booed off the stage. But life is full of boos, not just for comedians, and it's a sense of humour that gets you through the boos. And the *blues*, too."

The audience groaned at the pun.

"Sorry, couldn't resist. If you can't see the ridiculous side of things, it's awfully hard to deal with the serious side. A sense of humour may not be the secret of success, in other words, but I'm pretty sure it's the secret of life."

Max-Ernest glanced at Cass. She shook her head slightly, as if to say, *You're skating on thin ice with this secret stuff, buddy*, but he could see she was smiling.

"So here we are, about to graduate from middle school," he continued. "We've crossed one bridge, and we're about to cross another. Speaking of which, that reminds me of a joke—"

There were more groans. "No, don't do it!" "Spare us!"

Max-Ernest laughed. "You didn't really think I wouldn't tell one, did you? Actually, the joke I'm thinking of is the oldest joke in the book: why did the chicken cross the road? You all know the answer: to get to the other side. But think about it – that isn't really an answer; it's a statement of the obvious. In a sense, it's a restatement of the question. That's why it's funny. But that's also why it's mysterious."

He paused, slowing himself down. The one piece of advice Mrs. Johnson had given him was not to read too quickly.

"On some level, we don't really know why we do anything. Even less do we know where we're going. What lies on the other side of the road? We don't know until we get there. As the saying goes, it's not the destination, it's the journey. Whatever lies on the other side of the road, even if there's nothing much there at all, I've learned a lot along the way – from all of you. And now, like the rest of you, I'm getting out of here and I'm going to go take my act on the r—"

As he pronounced that last word, his voice cracked. Not so much from emotion, I'm afraid, but in that way that the voices of boys Max-Ernest's age so often do. Max-Ernest's voice was changing at the very moment he was finding it.

"Road," he squeaked out.

Nobody laughed at him this time. Not so much because they were being nice, but because they had tears in their eyes. So did he.

"I'll miss you all," said Max-Ernest.

And he walked off the stage to a standing ovation.

Amid the tears and applause, nobody noticed as Amber slipped away from her seat on the edge of the benches – least of all her parents. Nor did they see her climbing into the limousine that waited just outside the school gates.

Ms. Mauvais welcomed her with barely a nod, then waved to the driver with her gloved hand.

In silence, they drove off in search of a never-setting sun.

EPILOGUE

P. B.

Well, what did you think of my speech? Not bad for a kid, right?

I know, I know, I should never have started a sentence with *As the saying goes*. (If you ever give a graduation speech, please stay away from that awful phrase.) But all in all...?

Oh, what's that? It's not the speech – you're just surprised to hear me admit it outright? You mean admit that I, a man of such vast wisdom and experience – not to mention wit, intelligence, taste and discernment – that I, your not-so-humble narrator, Pseudonymous Bosch, *I* was young once, too?

Ah, well. You knew it all along anyway.

The story of how that boy became this man – I am not going to tell it now. (But if you can string together the words *volcano*, *ambidextrous*, *rhinoceros*, *spiderweb*, *mucus*, and *swim* – then, my friend, you are a much more inventive writer than I.) And I'm sorry to disappoint you, but I'm not going to tell you any more about the lives of Cass or Yo-Yoji or anybody else, either. Not right now.

I want to protect what little is left of their privacy; the Midnight Sun, as you know, is still at large, and our friends are still in danger. But I also want to protect something else: your imagination.

Think: do you really like it when a book or a movie

tells you what happens to characters after the end of a story? I don't like it at all. Usually, I get the feeling that the author or filmmaker is just making up the characters' fates on the fly. Is that really what happened? I wonder. Or did he just want to wrap up everything in a nice, tidy package?

In my experience, life rarely proceeds so neatly. It has a tendency to go off in all sorts of unexpected directions. Which is exactly where I like it to go.

As the saying goes, there's another side to every story. (Oops! Well, as that other saying goes, do as I say, not as I do.) If you take anything away from our time together, other than a toothache from all that chocolate, I hope it's the sense that what lies on the other side of a story is always a surprise.

Whether the other side itself is the Secret or whether the Secret is on the other side is a distinction without a difference. Either way, there's a new secret to discover.

The Secret is in your hands now. Don't let anyone spoil the ending.

—PB

If you are a "friend" of mine from
www.keepthesecret.co.uk, here's my very final
message to you: Abmpbqr cpfbkaq, vb emtb yljb rl
reb bka. Ilkd iftb reb Rbpybq Qlyfbrx! Mka jmx xls,
lsp kbv qbypbr hbbnbpq, ub uibqqba vfre mii lc reb
yelylimrb, mka klkb lc reb jmxlkkmfqb.
Cmfrecsiix xlspq, NU.

ALRIGHT – I ADMIT IT – YES!
THERE <u>ARE</u> MORE HEINOUSLY
ADDICTIVE BOOKS IN THE SECRET SERIES...

BUT READ THEM AT YOUR OWN RISK!

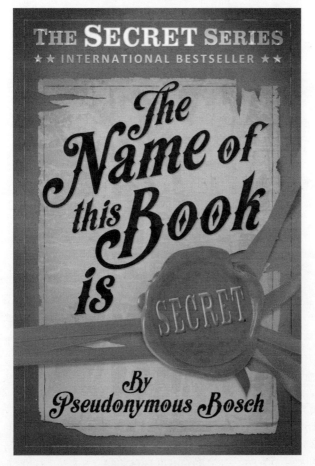

THE **SECRET** SERIES
★ ★ INTERNATIONAL BESTSELLER ★ ★

The
Name of
this Book
is

SECRET

By
Pseudonymous Bosch

ISBN: 9781409583820
EPUB: 9781409546214 KINDLE: 9781409546221

www.thenameofthisbookissecret.co.uk

SERIOUSLY, I CAN'T BE HELD RESPONSIBLE
IF YOU INSIST ON READING THE SECOND BOOK
IN THE SECRET SERIES...

THE SECRET SERIES
★ ★ INTERNATIONAL BESTSELLER ★ ★

If You're
Reading
This, it's
too Late

By
Pseudonymous
Bosch

ISBN: 9781409583837
EPUB: 9781409554691 KINDLE: 9781409554707

www.ifyourereadingthisitstoolate.co.uk

IF YOU BRAVED THE FIRST TWO BOOKS, YOU FACE
YOUR BIGGEST CHALLENGE YET WITH THE THIRD...
TRUST ME.

THE SECRET SERIES
★ ★ INTERNATIONAL BESTSELLER ★ ★

This Book is Not Good for You

By Pseudonymous Bosch

ISBN: 9781409583844
EPUB: 9781409554714 KINDLE: 9781409554721

www.thisbookisnotgoodforyou.co.uk

YOU'RE STILL HERE? ARE YOU <u>SURE</u> YOU'RE BRAVE
ENOUGH TO READ THE FOURTH BOOK IN THE (INCREDIBLY)
SECRET (BUT ALSO EXCELLENT) SERIES?

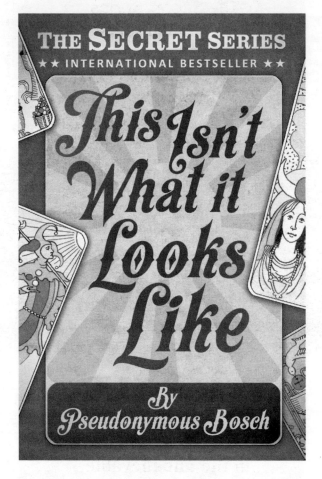

ISBN: 9781409583868
EPUB: 9781409554738   KINDLE: 9781409554745

www.thisisntwhatitlookslike.co.uk

What?
The Secret Series
isn't enough for you?
Then look out for more
from the pen of PB...

BAD MAGIC

An extraordinary new series
that will make you believe
in the unbelievable.

Coming soon

For P

WITH SECRET THANKS TO SB, JH, AND MP
AND TO MY MOM, WHO STILL HELPS ME WITH MY HOMEWORK

THIS EDITION FIRST PUBLISHED IN THE UK IN 2014 BY USBORNE PUBLISHING
LTD., USBORNE HOUSE, 83-85 SAFFRON HILL, LONDON EC1N 8RT, ENGLAND.
WWW.USBORNE.COM
FIRST PUBLISHED IN THE UK IN 2012.

A CIP CATALOGUE RECORD FOR THIS BOOK IS AVAILABLE FROM THE BRITISH
LIBRARY.
FMAMJJASOND/15   02816/10 ISBN 9781409583868
PRINTED IN CHATHAM, KENT, UK.